A Boarding House Adv

The Secret of the Old House
Meg Ashley

Regal Books

A Division of GL Publications
Ventura, CA U.S.A.

DEDICATION
To the 1982 graduating class of Orange Coast
Christian School

Published by Regal Books
A Division of GL Publications
Ventura, California 93006
Printed in U.S.A.

Library of Congress Catalog Card No.
Ashley, Meg, 1948-
    The secret of the old house.

    Summary: When Beth and her mother inherit an old farmhouse in
the Idaho woods, they decide to renovate and take in boarders
unaware that two different people are determined not to let them
occupy the house.
    [1. Mystery and detective stories]
I. Title.
PZ7.A82643Se 1982   [Fic]   82-13158
ISBN 0-8307-0845-6

CHAPTER 1

The white Cadillac bumped over the rain-rutted road. Mr. Osborne cursed beneath his breath as he swerved to miss a hole.

"I really don't think this trip is necessary, Mrs. Cooper. I told you the farm is rundown. The house oughta be leveled. You should just let me sell the place for you and you take the *money* for your inheritance."

The dark-haired, delicately-featured woman in the front seat continued staring out the car window. The trees alongside the road were winter bare. They stood in clumps as though they longed for company.

"My husband grew up in the house. I have to at least *see* it," she replied firmly.

They rounded a corner and the trees thinned. The misty rain cleared for a moment. The old, two-story farmhouse stood before them in the circle of sunlight breaking through the clouds.

The eleven-year-old girl in the backseat of the car leaned forward for a better view.

"Looks like it could be haunted," she said, her eyes twinkling.

"Oh, Beth! Don't be silly," her mother scolded. "That was Grandpa Cooper's house. It's *ours* now."

Mr. Osborne brought the car to a stop on what was once the front lawn, now overgrown with weeds, and slowly being reclaimed by the forest. "I suppose you have to see the insides too," he muttered as he began the painful process of pulling his huge belly out from under the steering wheel.

Rotten planks of wood on the front porch broke beneath the man's weight. Beth giggled and her mother gave her a threatening look.

The front door opened into what was once an elegant parlor. A marble mantelpiece and carved moldings around the ceiling spoke of the grace the room once knew. Now the faded wallpaper hung loose from the walls and the hardwood floor was covered with dust.

"Wow!" Beth whispered. She eased her way around Mr. Osborne's corpulent figure. Doors on either side of the room beckoned her. She wandered through the parlor into another big, empty room—a living room once, perhaps. More doors—the house was full of corners, halls and little nooks.

Beth glanced back at her mother talking with the real estate man in the parlor. She walked into another room. A large light fixture still hung in the center of the empty space. She decided to open the little door set in the corner. It opened into a narrow staircase that went up to the second floor. Shivering with excitement, the skinny little redhead began to climb the narrow steps.

Cobwebs hung from the ceiling. Beth climbed slowly. She could barely see her way in the dim light. Outside rain clouds were closing together in the sky and soon there would be no light left to explore by.

She hesitated on the landing at the top of the stairs, trying to decide which door to try next. The wood door on her right was bigger than the others. She pushed it open and stuck her curly head into the room.

"Musta been Grandpa's storage room," she whispered. Her voice seemed to disturb the still, heavy air. Boxes and crates lined the unpainted walls. A rusty set of bedsprings leaned against one wall. Beth spotted a small old-fashioned organ pushed back between some trunks at the far end of the room. Something about the instrument looked strangely out of place. It was the only thing in the room that wasn't covered with dust and cobwebs. She pushed her way through the collection of trunks and boxes to get a closer look. That's when she saw it.

Standing before her in the dim light, a huge wolf-like animal tensed, the low growl in his throat rising to an ominous snarl. Beth gasped and tried to back away. The animal moved toward her, his lips curled back from gleaming fangs, eyes shining with a savage light. Then Beth fell. She struck her head sharply and the room began to whirl around her. As she slipped beneath the wave of darkness, she thought she heard a voice, sounds of a struggle, then all was quiet.

When Beth regained consciousness, the animal was gone. There was no trace of it anywhere.

"Mom!" she gasped. She looked around frantically and felt her face for blood. There was none.

"Mom!" she screamed this time, and heard footsteps running up the stairs.

"What's wrong?!" Mrs. Cooper cried as she burst into the room. "Beth! Whatever happened?" She found her daughter and held her.

Mr. Osborne wheezed his way into the room and leaned his weight against the door frame. He began mopping his brow.

"It—it was a wolf, I think," Beth stammered. "It was there—" she pointed.

Mrs. Cooper looked around the room dubiously. "Sure you're not seeing those ghosts you expected?"

"Mom, honest—"

"It was probably just some stray that came in from the storm," Mr. Osborne interjected, dismissing the issue. "I'm sure it ran out. This place has been empty so long it's probably a haunt for all kinds of varmints."

Beth got up slowly, looked around and shook her head, disagreeing with his conclusions.

Mr. Osborne went on, "This part of Idaho is really no place for a widow woman, if you don't mind me saying so, regardless of this inheritance business." He pulled at his pale green jacket, trying to close it around his stomach. "Like I said, I've got a real good offer on this parcel of land. 'Course, the house isn't worth anything, but if you're interested in getting clear of the land—"

"We don't want to sell Grandpa's house!" Beth exclaimed, in spite of her recent scare. She looked at her mother. "What'd we drive all the way up here for if we were just going to sell it?"

Mrs. Cooper bit her lip. Her face was lined with worry. "This *is* the house where my husband was raised," she explained to the white-haired realtor. "There is something to be said for keeping it in the family. Why, the town was *named* for Grandpa Cooper! This is the oldest house in the area. It would be a shame not to keep it in the family."

"Well, this is a far cry from the life you're used to," Osborne grunted. "Life's harder up here, not all beach parties and fashion shows."

"And you're certain we can't adjust!" Mrs. Cooper said tersely, finishing his thoughts for him.

Mr. Osborne looked pointedly at her designer clothing and raised his eyebrows.

"This house isn't *either* worthless," Beth grumbled. She ignored Mr. Osborne's scowl and leaned against her mother's shoulder. "It's big and full of rooms. Besides," she added carefully, "there's that barn out back. I could have a horse, maybe, someday. Couldn't I?" She looked up at her mother hopefully. "You said you needed a change in your life now that Daddy's gone," she reminded gently.

Virginia looked uncertainly about her. "I need time, sweetheart. I've got to think this through. It's a big move from Los Angeles to the backwoods of Idaho." She pushed some of Beth's curls back from her forehead. "If I was certain we'd be happy—"

"This place needs a man to look after it!" Mr. Osborne stated as his final word on the subject. He turned around and walked down the hall to a second staircase, a wider one, that led down into the parlor. Beth and her mother followed slowly, looking into each of the bedrooms that opened off the hall. Each one was different; each had a feeling all its own.

When they arrived downstairs, Beth wandered around the parlor once more. "There sure is something special about this room!" she said.

Virginia stood still as though listening. "We could put the piano over there near the fireplace."

Mr. Osborne grunted in disgust and pulled his hat farther down on his head. He walked briskly outside into the drizzle. Virginia grinned at Beth and escorted her outside. They stepped gingerly across the sagging porch. When Virginia stepped off, her high heels sank into the damp earth.

"Just think, Mom! I could scream and yell out here all day and nobody'd ever care!" Beth whirled around, her face up to the rain. "Don't you just love it?!"

Just then one of Virginia's heels sank deeper in the mud and broke off as she tried to step. She groaned and began digging in the mud to retrieve it. "Yeah, it's just great!" she replied.

Before she got into the car, Beth turned for a last look at the old house. She didn't even see the faded, graying paint and the blatant signs of disrepair. It was the most beautiful house she'd ever seen.

She looked up at the windows of the second floor and felt her face again. How could she have imagined anything so real? But if there really was a wolf dog, where had he gone? Why wasn't she all chewed up? She tucked her questions away for another day and got into the car.

A lanky thirteen-year-old boy crouched in a tube-like crawl space that ran under the eaves from the storage room. He had his hand around the wolf dog's muzzle.

"You stupid dope," he scolded hoarsely. "You're a big help! It was just a girl!" He let go of the dog's mouth and the animal licked the boy's face playfully.

The boy crawled beneath the eaves to a tiny room at the other end. "Come on, Furball," he whispered. The dog came out of the crawl space into a tiny, unfurnished room. The boy replaced the false back of the cupboard that hid its opening. Then carefully he tiptoed across the bare floor to a crude door. At the sound of a car starting he sighed in relief. He beckoned his dog and they went out the door and down another set of stairs, this one broken and unpainted, ending in the woodshed. The woodshed was like another room of the house, a thoughtful addition. Not only was the firewood kept dry, but it was more easily accessible from the kitchen than if it was piled outside in the cold.

The boy went around a pile of wood stacked on the rough plank floor to where a trapdoor stood open, hidden from view. He pushed a lock of sandy-colored hair out of his eyes and grabbed

Furball around the belly. He climbed down a ladder that was attached to the wall of the underground tunnel and let the animal go. Furball ran ahead into the darkness and the boy followed, sure of the way.

Minutes later, they reached the other end of the underground passageway. The boy boosted his dog up out of the hole, then climbed out himself. He was now in a near-empty tack room set in a corner of the broken-down barn. A few bales of musty hay were piled near the trapdoor. The saddles and bridles that once decorated the walls were long gone, leaving only a faint scent of leather behind.

The boy gave his dog a gentle cuff and closed the trapdoor. He kicked some straw and dirt over the ring in the floor then checked to see if the yard was empty. Seeing no one, he raced for the woods, the dog close by his side.

The storm continued without a break into the night. Thunder seemed to rattle the darkness. By midnight, the dropping temperature had turned the rain to sleet. A low-flying plane winged its way south across the Canadian border. The two men in the cockpit were quiet; then the pilot peered into the storm and swore softly in French. They had no lights running on the plane. They could not risk being detected.

As a crack of thunder exploded around them, the pilot fought desperately for control. Ice and sleet made the plane slow to respond and they were flying dangerously low. The left wing tipped and struck a tree. The plane spun and dipped and plunged into the forest; a fire was burning in the midsection, a lonely torch in the black storm.

In a little house, three miles from the Cooper farm, a burly, slovenly man sat chewing on a wad of tobacco, reading a racing form intently. Vince Daggett, ex-lumberjack, heard the plane fly overhead. Minutes later, when he heard the crash, he knew it had gone down nearby. He threw down the paper and tossed his beer can into the kitchen. It hit the overflowing trash bag and rolled off. The last traces of beer dripped on the dirty floor. A polished piano standing in a corner of the living room looked incredibly out of place in the clutter.

Daggett strode down the hall and banged on his son's bedroom door. "Come on, Joey," he ordered. "There's been a plane crash. We'd better go see what's up."

Joey rubbed sleep from his eyes and hurriedly pulled on his clothes. "Come on, Furball," he called to his big dog, then followed his father out into the icy cold night. November was winter in the north woods of Idaho.

The trio made their way to the site of the airplane's crash, led by the glow of the flames. Joey shivered despite his sheepskin coat.

When they reached the wreckage, the boy stopped, horrified. Sections of metal lay strewn about. Fire licked the torn metal where fuel had spilled out. Vince moved the wad of tobacco in his mouth and went to some suitcases he spotted lying under a torn wing. Joey got control of himself and ran to the cabin of the craft. The pilot moaned in the cockpit.

"Dad, C'mere quick! One of 'em's still alive!" he

called out frantically.

Vince didn't answer. He was staring at the contents of one of the suitcases. Inside were neatly packaged sacks of white powder.

"Dad, we gotta get him outa here," Joey cried from inside the airplane. "He's stuck."

Vince tasted the substance in one of the sacks. His eyes filled with a strange light.

"Coke," he whispered. "Cocaine!" He licked his lips and quickly shut the suitcase. There were three more suitcases the same size.

"C'mere, boy," Vince called sharply. He spat out a stream of brown juice. "Take these two cases up to the lane."

"But, Dad, that man—" Joey protested.

Vince backhanded the boy sharply across the face. "Do as I say!" he shouted. The dog growled deep in his chest but stayed away from the man's heavy boots.

Joey held his throbbing jaw, dazed by the blow. Tears smarted in his eyes. He looked at his father in horror and disbelief. Then without a word he grabbed the two heavy cases and started for the lane. Vince did the same with the other two cases. They hurried away from the plane as the fire crept further along the fuselage.

Joey staggered under the weight of his load. When the plane exploded, he dropped the cases and turned to run back. Vince stepped to block his way, dropping his suitcases.

Joey pushed against his father and screamed, "They're gonna die!"

Vince held the boy's arms in a vise-like grip. "So what? They're smugglers—drug smugglers—"

"And we're murderers!" Joey sobbed, still struggling to get out of his father's grasp.

Vince laughed, then shook Joey. "Don't you know what's in them suitcases? Cocaine, boy! Lots of it! Hundreds, thousands, maybe a million bucks worth!!" Vince sounded happy. Joey looked at him incredulously.

"We're gonna be rich, son," Vince went on, "filthy rich! All we gotta do is find a buyer." He let Joey go. The boy stood still, looking at the blaze back in the woods. He knew it was too late now to help those men in the plane.

"Come on," Vince ordered, picking up his suitcases. "You gotta help me hide this stuff. You kin sure bet it's gonna be missed."

Joey stumbled along to where his suitcases lay in the snow. He struggled with the load and followed as best he could behind his father.

In Cooper's Creek the next morning, Virginia and Beth sat in Mr. Osborne's well-furnished office. Cooper's Creek was a very small town. Its one main street boasted two bars, a small combination grocery and drug store, a barber shop, a cafe, a branch office of a bank, Osborne's real estate office, a garage, a tiny post office and one church.

"We've decided to stay," Virginia told the realtor. "I've always wanted to fix up an old house like that, and now that I've inherited one, I'm going to do it! It's going to be a beauty. Besides," she glanced at Beth, "I think a change might be good for both of us."

Osborne rubbed his chin and tried to hide his

disappointment. He'd had his percentage from the sale of the Cooper farm all figured out.

"I surely do hope you're making the right decision, ma'am. I've never heard of a widow lady homesteading up here in the north woods."

"And I'm getting a horse!" Beth piped in smugly.

Mrs. Cooper ignored her daughter's interruption. "I called a lawyer friend in Los Angeles and instructed him to accept an offer we've had on our house there. He's also having our things packed and shipped to us. I guess all that's left is to get the house fixed up." She sighed happily. "Now if I could have those court papers to sign—"

"Humph!" Mr. Osborne grunted in disgust and shoved the papers across his desk. When their business was done, he forced a smile and escorted them to his door. "If you should change your minds, just let me know. I'm always ready to help."

Beth shook herself as she stepped out on the sidewalk. "Yuck," she whispered.

Mrs. Cooper stood beside her daughter and together they breathed deeply of the crystal pure air. The sleet from the night storm was melting and the ground was muddy in the warmth of the sunshine. Beth rolled down her window as soon as she got into their grey Audi sedan.

"Can we go back out to the house?" she asked, and flashed her mother her most winning smile.

Virginia pursed her lips. "Why not?" she said with a laugh. They drove north on the highway then, several miles out of town, turned off on a dirt road and followed it into the woods. When they turned onto a second dirt road, the rear wheels sank deep into the mud.

Virginia moaned and gave the car plenty of gas. She twisted the wheel, trying to get the car back on solid ground. The back wheels dug in deeper. She put the car in reverse, but it was useless. They were stuck.

The car seemed to be sitting in a lake of mud. Beth checked to see her mother's temper and gave her an encouraging grin. Then she slipped off her shoes and rolled up her pants' legs. Mrs. Cooper grumbled and followed Beth's example. When they stepped out into the muck, the mud oozed up through their toes. They began walking back toward the highway, carrying their shoes with them. Beth wisely ignored her mother's terse remarks.

"When do you figure we can look for a horse, Mom?" she asked dreamily. "I bet there's hundreds of them around here. Don't you wish we had one right now?"

Virginia didn't answer.

"I'm going to need a saddle and bridle and all that stuff. Can we get it at the same time?"

They were startled when a car pulled up behind them. Lights on top of the car told them it was the sheriff. The car stopped as it drew alongside. A rugged-looking, uniformed man with a brown moustache leaned out the window.

"The edge of the road's always the muddiest," he commented. He noted the fur jacket and tailored slacks the woman wore and shook his head.

Beth giggled. "I bet we look funny," she said.

Virginia pretended she hadn't heard.

"Would you like a ride back to town?" Sheriff

Larsen asked. "I noticed your car back there."

"Sure!" Beth answered, for both of them. "Can I sit in the back seat like a crook?"

The man smiled and got out to open her door. "I'm Paul Larsen, ma'am, sheriff," he said to Virginia. "You must be the lady from California who inherited the old Cooper place." He helped Virginia into the car.

"How'd you know?" Beth chirped from the backseat. She stuck her nose through the metal grill separating the backseat from the front.

The sheriff started the car and radioed back to Cooper's Creek for the tow truck.

"There's not too many folks in town who don't know what's going on around here. There's not much else to do besides keep track of other people's business."

"Yes, we're the Coopers," Virginia admitted. "The farm belonged to my late husband's father. We're the only kin left. We're planning to renovate the house," she added.

" 'Resurrect' would be a better word for it," the sheriff remarked. "I was headed out there myself, if you want to come along. By the way," he said, "you turned the wrong direction back there."

"Why're you going out to our place?" Beth asked.

Paul told them about the low-flying plane that had crashed during the storm in the night. "I was out there this morning at dawn with the ambulance. There were two men caught in the cabin when it exploded."

"We're not close to any landing fields, are we?" Virginia asked, puzzled.

"No," Paul answered, and seemed to close up.

"Well then, what were they doing, flying so low?" Beth asked, oblivious to Paul's signals that the conversation was over.

"I don't know," he answered tightly. "That's what I intend to find out."

CHAPTER 2

Vince Daggett stomped into his house and threw his wet coat across the sagging couch. It was Saturday morning and Joey was sitting at the piano, playing it softly. His shirt-sleeves were inches too short for his arms. He jumped to his feet. The dog, half German shepherd and half wolf, snarled openly at the man and Vince swore as he landed his heavily booted foot in its stomach. Furball yelped and crept back under the piano bench. Joey flinched but bit back his words.

"You sure nobody kin find that stuff?" Vince asked the boy gruffly.

Joey shrugged. "Nobody can find that crawl space unless he knows where to look."

"You sure better be right. This here's the best

thing ever happened to me. We got ourselves a gold mine!"

"Dad, why don't we just get rid of it?" Joey pleaded. "You've told me how bad drugs are."

"So what?" Vince replied. "We're not gunna snort it; we're gonna SELL it!" He laughed at the thought.

Joey stood behind the piano looking at his father.

Vince cursed. "What're you starin' at me like that for?"

Joey shook his head and struggled for words.

"You think I should jes' walk away from this?!" Vince asked angrily. "A million bucks drops in my lap and you want me to look the other way? *I'm* not gonna sell it to kids, ya know."

Joey turned back to the piano and ran his fingers across the shiny wood. "That's where it'll end up though—and we'll be to blame."

"Augh!" Vince growled. "Ye'r jes' like yer ma! I can't help it what other people do! I ain't responsible fer them."

Joey stood with his back to his father. Vince turned in disgust and went to the kitchen.

"Are you going to sell it around here?" Joey asked carefully.

Vince slammed the refrigerator door shut. "There ain't that much money in Cooper's Creek. I gotta find somebody with money, lotsa money!"

Vince grabbed an apple off the kitchen table. He took a bite out of it then spat the mushy pulp out on the floor.

"There ain't nuthin' around here fit to eat!" he complained and threw the apple across the room in disgust. It spattered on the piano keys.

Joey jumped as though he'd been struck. Vince turned and left the house, slamming the door behind him. As Joey heard the rickety pickup truck start up and drive away, he clenched his fists. He fought down the grief welling up inside him.

"Oh, Mom, when are you coming back for me?" he whispered. He started wiping off the piano keys with his shirt-sleeve. His teeth clenched in an effort not to cry.

Daggett's truck splashed through the puddles down the main street of town. He pulled up in front of Cooper's Creek Realty. Mr. Osborne, inside, saw the truck and groaned. He poured himself a quick drink from a bottle on his desk, then hid the glass and the bottle in a drawer. He had his smile in place by the time Daggett came through the door.

"Well, Vince, old friend, what brings you into town on such a fine day?" he asked warmly. "You want to place another bet? Tomorrow's race is going to be a big one!"

Vince ignored the man's outstretched hand. He sat down on one of the upholstered chairs and helped himself to a cigar.

Osborne winced as he looked at Daggett's filthy clothes.

"Siddown," Vince said, spitting the cigar tip on the carpet.

Osborne cleared his throat angrily. His smile was still in place, with much greater effort.

"You—ah, have something on your mind?"

Osborne asked, moving the cigars to a shelf.

"You still operate out of the restaurant up in Marble City?" Vince asked. He eyed Osborne through the cigar smoke.

"I don't know what business that is of—"

"Ain't," Vince replied. "I jes' want you to know that I know how big your little gamblin' operation is." Vince smiled at Osborne's discomfort.

"Gamblin' operation?"

"Never mind lyin'!" Daggett interrupted. "I wasn't thinkin' about saying anything to that sheriff fella. I jes' want you to know that I know about your added means of income, that's all."

"What do you want?" Osborne demanded. "Money? You never did like to work, so now it's blackmail—"

"As if you can talk," Vince snapped. "Bookie." He leaned forward in his chair. "No, Osborne, I don't want yer money. I want information and I figure you got it." He flicked his cigar ashes on Osborne's desk. "I'd jes' be real upset if my business got repeated anywheres else." Vince looked straight at Osborne. "If you know what I mean."

Osborne's shrewd eyes narrowed. "Information? What kind?"

"Markets," Vince replied. "A special kind of market, somebody who'd like to buy, say, a hundred kilos of cocaine."

Then Osborne's eyes bugged open. He swallowed and opened his desk drawer with a yank. He poured Daggett a generous drink and got another glass out for himself.

"One hundred kilos?" he repeated huskily.

Vince took a big drink of the whiskey and

coughed. "You heard me." he said.

"One hundred kilos," Osborne whispered, and began writing quick calculations on a pad of paper.

"This, ah, information you want, you're, ah, prepared to pay for it?"

"Twenty-five percent," Daggett replied, finishing off the liquor. "Take it or leave it." He stood up and strode to the door. "Jes' remember you've got nothin' to gain and lots to lose if you git a loose mouth."

Osborne was unaware of Daggett's departure. He was feverishly figuring his percentage. He wiped the sweat from his forehead and grabbed the telephone.

At the same time Vince Daggett was busy with Mr. Osborne, the Cooper's grey sedan was parked outside the Kootenai Cafe. Beth and her mother were sitting in a booth going through the local newspaper.

"Here's one, Mom!" Beth grabbed the ads section away from her mother. "A two-year-old filly," she read. "Twelve hands—"

"Twelve hands?" Virginia asked.

"High," a deep voice behind them explained.

The Coopers were startled to see the sheriff standing by their table. At first Beth didn't recognize Mr. Larsen in his faded blue jeans, plaid shirt, and worn boots.

"Oh, hi," Beth answered warmly. She looked quickly at her mother.

"Mind if I join you?" he asked, fiddling with his hat.

"Why—why no," Virginia said. "We were just looking at ads for horses. Beth seems to think that should be first on our list now that we've decided to stay. She has even convinced me to camp out at the house while it's being remodeled."

Paul shook his head. "Well, I guess I could loan you some camping equipment, if you're serious. But I think a motel would be more to your liking." Then he turned to Beth. "Do you know much about horses?"

"Sure—" "No!" Beth and her mother answered at the same time.

Paul smoothed down his thick moustache in an effort not to smile. Beth was wearing designer jeans and a velour top. Her boots looked brand new. Virginia still dressed as if she was modeling for a fashion magazine.

"I was planning to go down to Coeur d'Alene to a livestock auction this afternoon. It's as good a place as any to look for a horse. Would you like to go?"

"Super!" Beth answered. Then, as her mind kept working, "Are you bringing your kids too?

"My kids?" the sheriff laughed. Then he became serious. "My little girl lives a long ways away from here with her mother. She's about fourteen now, I guess." There was sadness in the sheriff's voice.

Virginia gave Beth a stern look. Paul saw it and smiled. "It's okay," he assured them. "I've been divorced long enough now to get used to being alone. My wife just never could adjust to country living."

Neither Beth nor Virginia could think of anything to say for a moment.

"Do you see your girl very much?" Beth asked, trying to make amends.

"Not as often as I'd like," the sheriff confessed. "But how about it? Are you interested in the auction or not?"

Virginia nodded. "Yes," she said. "We'd love to go."

The auction in Coeur d'Alene was a big operation. Livestock bellowed and neighed from a score of pens. Beth climbed up every corral fence she came to.

"Are you looking for a filly or a gelding?" Paul asked her after she'd looked awhile.

Beth thought for a moment, then smiled. "I really had my heart set on a palomino," she answered.

Paul choked on his laughter.

Beth looked at her mother. "What'd I do?"

Virginia put an arm around the girl's shoulders. "I'll explain it later," she said as she stepped carefully through the stockyard debris. "I guess we have a lot to learn," she said to Paul.

He looked down at her suede pumps and nodded. "Yes. Ah, you know this isn't exactly clean dirt around here, don't you?"

Virginia's eyes widened. She looked down at her soiled pumps and moaned.

Later, back in Cooper's Creek, Paul outfitted the Coopers with a carload of his camping equipment. Virginia called a halt when he brought out the tent.

"No way! I like a roof over my head!" She looked firmly at Beth. "We'll sleep *in* the house!"

Beth was still exuberant about the horse they'd bought at the auction and wasn't about to aggravate her mother. She smiled sweetly. "Fine with me!"

Paul slammed the trunk of the car shut. "There's plenty of nice motels in Coeur d'Alene when you change your minds," he said as his good-bye.

Monday afternoon when Paul delivered Nutmeg, Beth's roan mare, several other trucks were parked beside Cooper's house. A pair of men were on the roof replacing shingles. Virginia was talking to a dark-haired, lean young man when she saw Paul's truck and horse trailer drive up. She called over her shoulder to Beth.

The girl let out a screech from inside the house and ran out to help the sheriff with her horse. Nutmeg pranced and shied nervously. Paul held out the halter rope to Beth, but she backed away from the horse's dancing hooves.

"You go ahead," she offered. Paul led the mare into her stall in the barn and tied her there.

"I bet you've been around horses a lot," she said.

Since I was younger than you," he told her. "You did a good job of putting the straw down for her," he said, "but next time, not so much. About half will do fine."

Beth bit her lip in embarrassment.

"You know how to take care of her?" Paul asked bluntly.

Beth was about to answer yes when she met the

sheriff's piercing eyes. She shrugged.

"I—I just figured I'd feed her and ride her," she admitted.

"I thought so," Paul said. "Come on."

They went back to his truck and he handed the girl several brushes and a currycomb. He lifted out a small saddle, a saddle blanket and a bridle.

"I figured I'd lend you this tack until you get your own gear."

"Gee, thanks!"

"You have to promise me you'll take care of it," Paul added as he carried the things inside the barn and set them down on a bale of hay. "No leaving it lying around, you hear? And don't you ever unsaddle that horse without rubbing her down good!"

Beth nodded. "Yes, sir."

"Now, have you ever saddled a horse before?"

Beth shook her head and kicked the barn dust up into the sunlight.

Paul smiled and tousled her curly hair. "Okay, little Miss Cooper, let's learn."

While the lessons continued on in the barn, Virginia finished her tour through the house with the contractor. They decided to leave the old kitchen, with its cast-iron, woodburning stove, as it was. A modern, but smaller, kitchen would be built into one end of the long dining room.

After the planning was complete, Virginia pushed her hair back and sighed. "I guess that's it. It scares me a little to sink so much of my money into this place, but I guess it's a good investment." She laughed self-consciously. "I really don't know, though, what I'm going to do with myself way out here, once this renovating is finished."

Chuck Warren, the contractor, stuck his pencil behind his ear. He was a pleasant-looking man, younger than Virginia. His eyes gave him his distinction. They gave Virginia the feeling that he knew some secret that was about to send him into laughter or song.

"Have you ever considered taking in boarders, Mrs. Cooper? You have five big bedrooms upstairs and three downstairs." He smiled, "You'd have some income, and you might enjoy it."

"A boarding house? Would people want to come stay in a place like this?" She looked skeptical. "How on earth would anyone ever find out about us?"

"Referrals, advertising, word of mouth. I come in contact with a lot of people. In fact," he admitted, "I have someone in mind right now."

Virginia looked at him quizzically.

His eyes sparkled. "I guess I should tell you that I'm also the pastor of that little church in town. We're a very small congregation and I support myself doing contracting. Anyway," he went on, "my great-aunt is retiring from the mission field and she needs a place to live. I've never liked the thought of her living alone and she refuses to live with family. She's a funny old bird," he added.

Virginia was silent as she walked beside Chuck out to his truck. "I don't know," she confessed. "We're really just camping out here right now. Beth thinks it's great fun. She'll probably want to sleep out in the barn with her horse tonight."

"Well, the bedrooms don't need much besides

paint and wallpaper," Chuck said. "We'll have the new kitchen built in a couple of weeks. Think about it."

At that moment Nutmeg came trotting out of the barn with Beth bouncing along on top. She was holding onto the saddlehorn for dear life, but managed a quick wave to her mother.

"Look at me!" she yelled.

"Hold the reins, Beth," Paul shouted from the barn.

Beth managed to get the horse around the yard. She felt every jarring step the horse took. "I—thought—this—was—supposed—to be—fun," she managed to say between bounces.

After everyone else had left, and the horse was stabled for the night, Beth walked slowly and painfully back to the house with her mother. She wrapped her arm around her mother's waist for support.

"He's really nice, isn't he, Mom?"

"He who?"

"The sheriff, Mr. Larsen." Beth tried to sound casual.

"I suppose so," Virginia conceded. "But don't get any ideas, young lady. Your father was a very special man. He's a hard act to follow. Why do you think I've stayed alone so long? Besides, I've got enough problems right now with this house."

They walked up the back steps and into the kitchen. "You know, there *is* something about this old house," Virginia said. "She reminds me of myself somehow—sort of sad," Mrs. Cooper became silent, thinking.

"She's only sad 'cause she's empty," Beth said.

They were drawn to the warmth of the cast-iron stove. Autumn was much colder here than in California. Beth opened the door to the woodshed to get more wood.

Virginia warmed her hands over the stove. "You know, I'm going to enjoy seeing this old place come alive again," she admitted.

"I bet she gets happy too," Beth said, adding a chunk of wood to the blaze.

Her mother laughed. "Yes, I'll bet she does!"

Out in the woods, Vince Daggett's dark figure blended in with the rock behind him. He looked across the yard to the lights in the Cooper's house.

"You know what's going on in there?" Vince asked. Joey stood behind him, keeping a hand on Furball's head.

"Looks like somebody's staying there," Joey replied. "Maybe old Osborne finally sold out."

"I want you to go in later and check the stuff. As soon as I can figure out a good spot for it, we'll have to move it out of there." Vince stood up. "I don't want anything or anybody messing up this deal. You understand?"

Joey nodded sadly and looked away.

He and Furball huddled together to keep warm after Vince left. Joey waited until the lights in the house had been out a while before crossing the clearing to the barn. Nutmeg nickered when they entered the barn. Joey went to her stall.

He reached out and petted her. "You live here too, huh?" Furball nipped at Joey's leg. "Okay, okay, I'm coming." He stroked the horse one last time then headed for the tack room.

Once he was in the underground tunnel, he ordered Furball to stay. The dog whined, but obeyed. At the other end, Joey climbed up into the woodshed and then climbed up the stairs into the little room. Once he was in the crawl space, he beamed his flashlight on the sacks of white powder tucked between the wood studs of the wall.

"I wish I'd never told Dad about this place," he muttered. An overwhelming sense of loneliness drove him past the cocaine on into the storage chamber. He lay down on the rug and stared out the tiny window as he had done a hundred times before. The sky was so big—and silent. That dull ache was beginning to be at home in his chest.

Maybe this is what it means to grow up, he thought.

Joey got up and went to the old organ that stood against the wall. He carefully dusted off the few specks of dirt that marred its shiny wood surface. Then he sat down and deftly ran his fingers over the yellowed keys. He could hear the music in his mind. It was beautiful and good and made him want to cry. Maybe someday beauty wouldn't make him sad. He took a deep breath and swallowed the lump in his throat.

Before he left the big storage chamber he rummaged behind some crates and retrieved a shoe box. He lifted the lid off and glanced over the contents: a jackknife, a fishing fly, a couple of rocks and part of a photograph. It showed a woman playing a piano, singing. A little boy stood beside her, singing too.

He tucked the box under his arm, took a last look around and headed back through the crawl space. As he passed the poison he'd brought into the house, he felt as though he'd betrayed an old and precious friendship.

CHAPTER 3

The sound of another low-flying airplane shattered the stillness of the dawn. Beth woke with a start and ran out to the old kitchen to look. Her mother was already there, peering out the window. The plane seemed to be circling over something.

Vince and Joey enacted a similar scene, except Vince was compelled to investigate further. He pulled on his boots and grabbed his hat, coat and rifle. Joey watched him melt into the woods like an Indian.

The seaplane continued circling over the crash site of the other plane. Eventually it landed on the lake two miles west.

Vince played a hunch and stayed near the

crash site, crouched behind a thick stand of trees. After about twenty minutes he saw two men come near the clearing where the wreckage lay.

The taller of the two men smoked a dark brown cigarette while his partner rummaged through the debris.

"Of course it is not here!" the tall man snapped.

"But, Jacques, why is there no report of it, nothing in the news?" the shorter man protested.

"Because someone found it, just as I told you!" Jacques ground out his smoke with the heel of his boot. "It will turn up. We will notify our men to watch the outlets." He motioned his partner to follow. "Meanwhile we must stay and listen. You will get a room in Coeur d'Alene. I will find a place closer. We will find the fool who thinks he can play with our kind of fire."

Vince stayed hidden in the trees long after the men returned to their seaplane. "Well, you ain't gonna find it," he said to the departed men. "And you ain't gonna find me either!"

He stood to his feet, took off his hat and gave his thinning brown mat of hair a good scratch. "But I sure don't want it at my place, and I don't trust Osborne at all."

A sudden thought sent him gliding through the woods. He stood behind the big rock north of Cooper's place and watched as Beth hurried out to the barn.

Then Virginia came to the kitchen door and called her daughter. Beth ran from the barn and grabbed her mother's hand. They were laughing as they walked to the car, completely unaware of the threat that lurked so near.

"It's already in the best hidin' spot," Vince whispered. "Jes' them females 're in the wrong place."

Vince was headed back toward his own house when he saw two other vehicles coming down the road. They drove right up to the Cooper's house. Chuck Warren and his crew began unloading tools and heading to their various tasks. Vince spat and silently disappeared into the woods.

Beth and her mother spent the day their favorite way—shopping. Beth had chosen the northeast bedroom downstairs for her room. It had its own fireplace and a door to the outside that opened onto the front porch. There was also a huge walk-through closet that connected Beth's room with her mother's. The closet even had a regular-sized window in it that looked out on what would one day be the garden.

Both Beth and her mother wanted to make Beth's room special. In Coeur d'Alene they bought priscilla curtains for the multi-paned windows and ordered a thick beige rug to cover most of the hardwood floor. Beth picked out her own wallpaper, and in an antique shop they found an upholstered lounge chair and a floor lamp.

By noon they had the car loaded down with bags, boxes and rolls of wallpaper. They arrived home just in time to see the moving van from California back up to the front porch. Virginia was surprised that it had come so quickly.

By dusk the Coopers were alone again. The house looked more like a home now that all the furniture was there. Virginia sat at the baby grand piano in the parlor and played. The music seemed sad to Beth. She moved some boxes out of the way and stood, leaning on the piano, watching her mother's face.

"Mom," she said, "Mom, play that church song Daddy liked so much."

Mrs. Cooper looked up and gave Beth a wistful smile. The music changed. "It needs tuning, doesn't it?" she asked as she played.

Beth sang the words. "A mighty fortress is our God, a bulwark never failing . . ." She could see her mother's face relax as the song unfolded.

The room seemed to absorb the music and hold it in its walls. In the silence after the song, Beth felt the music still moving through the air. Even her mother sat listening in the quietness. Then Virginia broke the spell.

"Well, we have one more errand to do to make this day complete," Mrs. Cooper announced. "Groceries! The refrigerator is empty. Come along, Button. Our camping days are over."

Beth was drowsy as they drove home from town. She felt content leaning on her mom's shoulder, listening to Virginia softly singing the words of the hymn as they drove down the very dark country roads. Beth became alert when her mother stopped singing abruptly. Another set of headlights faced them on the narrow dirt road near their house. The headlights were high and almost blinding.

"A truck," Mrs. Cooper commented. "And it's coming awfully fast." She flicked her beams and slowed her speed. The truck bore down on the sedan as though the driver was unaware of them. Mrs. Cooper edged closer and closer to the side of the road. At the moment the truck should have passed them, Beth screamed, "He's going to hit us!"

Mrs. Cooper hit the horn and swerved off the road to avoid a collision. The truck barreled on into the night, not stopping, not caring what damage it had done.

The side of the road was filled with big rocks and shrubs. The Audi sedan bounced and jerked along as Mrs. Cooper fought to maneuver it back onto the road. Beth was afraid the car would flip over. She braced herself and prayed. A quarter of a mile later, the car finally got back where it belonged. Mrs. Cooper turned off the motor and sat for a moment, quieting her nerves. Beth leaned her head against the dashboard.

"You alright?" Mrs. Cooper asked, her voice husky with emotion.

Beth nodded. Her mother hit the steering wheel with her fist. "I'd sure like to meet the yahoo driving that thing!" she exploded. "Of all the dirty, rotten, lousy, ill-mannered and—dangerous stunts, that just about takes the cake!"

Mrs. Cooper kept fuming and sputtering until Beth started laughing.

"Mom," she gasped, "you look so funny!" She held her stomach and laughed some more. "I can just see you bawling out some big trucker!"

Mrs. Cooper chuckled too at the thought and restarted the car. "Well, whatever that joker meant to prove, he failed," she said emphatically.

Later, when Virginia sat on Beth's bed for their bedtime talk, Beth gave a sleepy, happy sigh. "Let's pray like we used to," she murmured.

Virginia stretched out on top of the covers. "Okay, dear, go ahead."

"Father in heaven," Beth began, "thank you for being here, and thank you for getting us back on the road again." Her "amen" was lost somewhere in sleep. Mrs. Cooper thoughtfully arranged Beth's curls on the pillow. Prayer had not been part of their lives for a long time.

"Amen," she whispered.

In the middle of the night, Beth was jarred awake. She was out of bed before she realized that the noise that woke her was the telephone's incessant ringing. She ran to the dining room and had to search for the phone amid all the boxes that still waited to be unpacked.

"Hello," she answered at last.

Silence—a long silence. Beth felt a chill run up her back. She was about to hang up when a deep voice growled, "Too bad 'bout tonight. There'll be more if you stay."

"Who was that?" Mrs. Cooper sleepily called from the living room.

"I don't know," Beth said. She hesitated. "Wrong number, I guess." She crossed her fingers so the lie wouldn't count.

The phone rang again hours later. Virginia beat Beth to it. Beth watched her mother's expression change from fear to disgust. After she hung up, she buried the telephone in a packing box full of padding.

"That's about enough of that," Virginia said. "We don't need any more wrong numbers tonight." She looked at Beth's guilty face and whacked the girl on the fanny. "Now get to bed."

Beth tried and tried to get back to sleep. She tried to remember how many doors the house had and gave up at five. She lay trembling in the dark. "God," she whispered, "you're going to have to take care of us. They have crazy people up here too."

The girl fell asleep wondering if angels still carry swords.

The next afternoon, a half-dozen workmen pounded, scraped, painted and polished. Chuck Warren, the contractor, found Mrs. Cooper in the small southeast bedroom, off the parlor, sorting through a pile of papers.

"This is what I get for not going home to do my own packing," she said. "I don't know where anything is."

Chuck sat down on a corner of the desk. "Have you thought about my suggestion at all?" he asked.

Virginia set down the files she was holding. "Yes, I have," she admitted. "Frankly, it scares me. I've gotten used to living alone with Beth. I don't know how I'd feel about having other people around all the time."

Chuck was about to say something, but Virginia hurried on. "But, I've also thought that, well, things are different now. This old house is big, and—used to being full of people. I'm not really even sure I *want* to be alone way out here." She looked up at the young pastor-contractor. "So, yes, tell your great-aunt that we'd love to have her."

"Great!" Chuck said, laughing. "When do you think you'll be ready for a second boarder?"

It was Virginia's turn to laugh. "You don't

waste any time, do you?"

Beth barged in just at that moment. "Mom, can I ride Nutmeg now? Can I? I've got all my stuff unpacked."

"Beth, say hello to Mr. Warren, like a lady," her mother admonished.

"Hi!" Beth said with a grin. "Can I, Mom, can I please?"

"Well, I guess so," Virginia said. "Can you saddle her by yourself yet?" she called after the girl.

"Sure!" was the answer hollered from the front porch as the door slammed shut.

"I've got to get that girl back in school," Virginia observed.

Chuck was still waiting for an answer to his question. "It would be a short-term boarder," he said. "Not more than two months."

"Well, who—whom did you have in mind?" Virginia asked as she kept on sorting through her papers.

"Her name's Shannon Dyer," Chuck said. "She's sixteen, from a wealthy family near Spokane. She, ah, well, she's pregnant, Mrs. Cooper, and she needs a place to stay until the baby's born."

Virginia listened incredulously. "You have to be kidding! You want me to take on that kind of problem?"

Chuck looked down at his calloused hands. "Yes, I kind of hoped you would. Her folks called me last week. This has been real hard on them. They asked if I knew someone who could keep her this last bit of time. They'll pay you well."

Virginia waved aside his last remark, "I'm not

concerned about the money," she said as she stood up. "Although I suppose I ought to be." She walked to the window and looked out. "What about Beth? How would this affect her? And, why, the girl's a minor. What about insurance and doctors—?"

"All those things can be taken care of quite easily," Chuck replied. "You know that. I guess the real question you have to answer is whether or not this is the kind of living you want to get involved in or not. I can't answer that question for you." He got to his feet. "The men have the floors done in the two north bedrooms upstairs. If you want us to move the furniture up, we can do that tomorrow."

Virginia still stood looking out the window. "Yes, that would be fine. I have some more things being delivered from town tomorrow that need to go upstairs too."

"You do need to consider Beth, Mrs. Cooper," Chuck admitted. "You can't protect her from the world with its sin. She needs to be allowed to face situations where she has to make some decisions. There are some compromises that cripple a person for life. How are you going to show her that?"

At that moment Virginia watched Beth proudly lead Nutmeg toward a special flat stone south of the house, from which she could mount the horse. As they walked, the saddle slowly began slipping around the horse until it hung under the mare's stomach. Nutmeg snorted and refused to go farther. Beth pulled on the reins with disgust until she noticed the problem.

Virginia saw her stomp her foot and kick a rock. The girl tried to fix the saddle but could not quite manage it. Finally Beth turned the horse around and led her back toward the barn.

"You're right," Virginia admitted. "I've been trying to shield Beth from every kind of pain ever since her father died. That last year of his life was, well, it was awfully hard on both of us." Virginia looked tired just remembering it. "But you're right, Chuck. I can't do it. She has to see life as it is—the good and the bad, and I guess I just have to pray to God that she'll make the right choices when it's her turn."

Mrs. Cooper faced the man who confronted her. "Tell the Dyers that Shannon may come."

Another talk was going on at Daggett's house. Mr. Osborne stood in the middle of Vince's living room, refusing to sit down on any of the soiled furniture.

"I found a man who can help us," he said.

Vince stood across the room. He noticed how Osborne's eyes kept moving around the room as though he was looking for something. He was glad Joey was at school.

"But," Osborne went on, "we need a bigger cut."

"I said you could take it or leave it," Vince repeated adamantly.

"Be reasonable," Osborne argued. "Why should we both get only twenty-five percent and you get the rest? We're taking a lot of the risks—"

"Because I've got the goodies, that's why!" Vince snapped. "You've got twenty-five percent of nothing unless you've got me!"

"Unless we find it and take it for ourselves," Osborne added, smiling. "One-hundred percent sounds much better to both my partner and me."

Vince started across the room. "You dirty—"

Osborne backed toward the front door. He held up his hands. "You could be persuaded to increase our cut—" He glanced over his shoulder at a car that was pulling up outside.

Something in Osborne's smile made Vince look over the man's shoulder. The car outside belonged to the sheriff's department. The short, stocky, uniformed man getting out of the car was Jake Moran, the deputy sheriff.

CHAPTER 4

Beth started in at the local school the next Monday. No one seemed very friendly, and compared to the junior high she had been attending back in L.A., the place was a dump. The hours dragged by.

Beth dreaded the long walk home from the bus stop. Two girls that got off with her headed home in a different direction. Only a tallish older boy in scruffy clothes was going in Beth's direction. By walking very quickly, she only just managed to keep up with his long strides.

She screwed up her courage. "Hi, I'm Beth, Beth Cooper. I live in that old house up ahead."

The boy kept his head down. "Hi," he mumbled. Beth kept after him. Finally he admitted his name was Joey Daggett.

At the junction where they turned onto the narrow gravel road that ran past both of their homes stood a big dog. Joey whistled and the wolf-like animal ran to meet him. Beth gasped and tensed as she watched the dog loping toward them.

"How ya doing, Furball?" Joey said. He dropped his books and tussled happily with his pet.

"Furball? Furball?" Beth repeated. "Hey, you! You were up in that room!"

Joey stood up and put a hand on the dog's head to quiet him. Beth was remembering it all now.

"That's the—the beast that attacked me, isn't it?" She advanced toward the boy, her anger demanding an explanation. Furball curled back his lips. A snarl rumbled in his throat.

Joey held the dog back. "Yeah, it was us. We didn't mean any harm. He just protects me, that's all. He thought you were a threat—like now."

Beth stopped at the sight of the dog's fangs.

"He won't hurt you if he's your friend. Honest." Joey knelt down by the dog. "This is Beth, Furball. She's our neighbor. It's okay, boy. She won't hurt us." He looked up at the girl. "See? Come here—let him smell your hand."

"You're sure he won't bite it off?"

"Sure, I'm sure. Come on."

Beth reached out slowly and stroked the dog's muzzle. He allowed the touch. She scratched behind his ears and petted his thick fur.

"I like him a lot better this way," she admitted. "But, Joey, where'd you go that day? You guys just disappeared."

Joey got quickly to his feet and became very

distant again. "I—I have a place. I used to go there—when the house was empty. I don't come anymore."

"What do you mean, a place?" Beth persisted.

"It's where—it's where I kept my snake, my pet snake Herman. He's still there in that room somewhere. You really ought to be careful; he hates strangers even more than Furball."

The word "snake" slowed Beth down.

"You mean there's a snake in our house?"

"Oh, he won't bother anybody—he's in that storage room. That's where he lives. I bet you'll never see him unless you go poking around in there."

Joey started walking away.

"Hey," Beth called after him, "why don't you come to my house and show me that place? Herman knows you!"

Joey ignored her invitation.

"My mom makes real good pies!"

Joey just kept striding away. Beth shrugged her shoulders and trudged on home. "Boys are weird," she concluded.

As she neared her house, she saw Chuck Warren, the contractor-pastor, helping an old lady out of his truck. Beth took a good look at the old woman.

"Oh brother," she moaned softly. The lady was smallish, but stood ramrod-straight. Her gray hair was done up in braids that were wrapped around her head. She was wearing a black shapeless dress and old granny-style shoes. She even had a shawl around her shoulders and wire-rimmed spectacles on her nose.

"She sure looks like a lot of fun," Beth commented as she walked up to where her mother was standing.

"You hush," Virginia whispered sternly.

"Mrs. Cooper," Chuck said, "I'd like you to meet my great-aunt, Stella Evans. Auntie, this here is Virginia Cooper and her daughter Beth.

While Virginia ushered the old lady into the house, Beth escaped to the kitchen. She was doing her homework on the dining room table when Miss Evans came down the narrow stairs.

Beth's mouth hung open. The only thing she recognized about the woman was her spectacles. Miss Evans had changed into faded blue jeans—not a designer fit, Beth could see, but definitely blue jeans. She had on white tennis shoes and wore a man's flannel shirt with the sleeves rolled up to her elbows.

The old woman smiled at Beth's astonishment. "I kept a few things out of the missionary barrels for when I retired," she explained. "Is snacking between meals allowed around here?"

Beth took a moment to find her voice. "Yeah, sure. There're some cookies in the dishwasher."

"In the dishwasher?" Miss Evans looked with new interest at the girl.

"Yeah, Mom tries to hide them from me. Here, I'll get you some."

The old lady tucked a couple of cookies in her pocket and wandered off toward the parlor, munching happily.

Beth stared after her. "Weird," she whispered. "Really weird."

The second boarder arrived the following Saturday. Beth was out in the barn brushing Nutmeg when she heard a car pull up. She walked out to the front yard to get a peek at the "problem" her mother said was coming.

Shannon Dyer stood by the car, her arms crossed over her bulging tummy, staring at the ground. She had a chic hairstyle that Beth envied and she wore her expensive-looking outfit carelessly.

Chuck Warren again acted as the bellhop and carried the girl's bags up the steps and into the house. Shannon did not follow him.

Beth walked out to meet their new guest. She introduced herself and held out her hand.

The teenager looked away in disgust. "You might as well know right off," she said, "that I didn't want to come here. This is another one of my father's brilliant ideas."

She walked up the steps of the porch. "What kind of place is this anyway? It sure doesn't look like much of a resort hotel to me."

Beth laughed nervously. "It isn't. We just moved in ourselves. We have so much room we thought we'd take in boarders. Pastor Warren told us about you."

Shannon leaned against the porch railing. "Yeah, I'll bet he did," she said. "Well, little girl, I don't want to be patronized. I don't want your pity and I don't care what you think about me. I just want to be left alone."

With that announcement Shannon let herself into the house and found the front staircase up to the second floor.

Beth shrugged her shoulders and walked back to the barn. She felt as though someone had just slapped her across the face.

Shannon glared at the two workmen who were painting the upstairs hall and looked around angrily at the different doors. She chose one at random and barged in.

Miss Evans was kneeling beside her bed, with an opened Bible on the bed before her. She was wearing baggy coveralls and a French beret. Her gray braids hung down her back. She looked up calmly at the intrusion.

"You must be Shannon," she said, rising slowly to her feet. "Well, welcome to the boarding house. Your room is across the hall. Come along and I'll show you."

Shannon was startled into silence and followed the queer little lady who led her away.

Shannon's room was done in colorful greens and browns. The comforter on the four-poster bed matched the light green of the thick carpet. It was a beautiful room, though, unlike Miss Evans's room, it didn't have its own fireplace. The antique furniture was a matched set. Shannon was unwillingly impressed. She walked to the windows, pushed aside the sheer white curtains and looked down into the backyard. A storm was brewing. The light outside was muted by the clouds overhead.

"Not bad, is it?" Miss Evans said. "Everyone's hoping you'll be happy here, dear."

"Well, I won't be," the girl replied without looking at the old woman. "And I'm not your dear."

Miss Evans raised an eyebrow. "Suit yourself,"

she replied and quietly left the room.

Shannon stood there, seeing nothing, until movement outside caught her eye. Beth was riding Nutmeg. At least she was on top of the horse. Nutmeg was going pretty much where she wanted to go. At the moment that happened to be toward a thick clump of dry grass in the middle of the backyard. Beth kicked the horse with her heels and pulled on the reins. She scolded Nutmeg with vigor.

Shannon smiled. She found the stairs that went down to the dining room and went past a couple of carpenters working on the new kitchen without saying a word to anyone. She walked out the back door and sat on the steps, watching Beth.

The girl had given up reasoning with her horse. Now she was ready to use force. She stood behind Nutmeg with a switch in her hand.

"When I tell you to giddiup, you better giddiup, you stupid—"

Shannon laughed. Beth's attention and anger shifted to the older girl.

"What's so funny?"

"You're something else!" Shannon called. "You hit her with that stick and you're going to get a hoof right in the mouth."

"Well, she won't go!" Beth cried in exasperation.

"Why should she? She knows who's boss."

Shannon walked to the animal and grabbed the bridle. "Here, I'll show you how it's done."

"Hey, get away from my horse," Beth ordered. She grabbed the reins back. "She's my horse and I'm the only one who rides her!"

Gusts of wind chilled them as they stood glaring at one another. Beth led Nutmeg back to the barn.

"I don't want to ride that bag of bones," Shannon called after her. "My father wouldn't have that nag on our ranch. If she was mine, she'd be in a glue bottle. That's where she belongs."

The cold war between the two girls continued through supper. Miss Evans wore a long lacy gown to the evening meal. "I've been saving this dress for years," she explained when she took her place at the table.

"I can tell," Shannon remarked.

Beth lurched her chair and managed to land a solid kick on Shannon's shin.

"Oh, sorry," she apologized sweetly.

When everyone moved into the parlor, the girls chose opposite sides of the room. Beth lay half under the grand piano, reading a book. Miss Evans sat in a corner in her rocking chair. The chair was her contribution to the parlor's furnishings. It didn't exactly fit the parlor decor, but Mrs. Cooper didn't know what to do about it.

Outside, rain poured down and sounded like sleet against the windows. Lightning and thunder broke simultaneously like an explosion. Shannon leafed nervously through a magazine. She disliked storms. "We own a dozen horses," she said loudly over the din of the storm to no one in particular. "Thoroughbreds. I ride every day."

"Oh, really?" Beth answered, trying to sound bored. The lights suddenly went out. They were all startled for a moment.

"I'll fetch a lantern," Mrs. Cooper said. "I think

Sheriff Larsen's is still in the kitchen somewhere."

The flickering light from the fireplace cast shadows on the walls.

"Yes," Shannon went on nervously, "I've been in several shows. I have ribbons at home."

Beth's teeth grated. "It must be hard on you not to be riding anymore."

Shannon glared. "Oh, I could ride if I wanted to; the doctor said so—as long as I'm careful."

"Not here, you can't," Beth said, gloating. "You don't have a horse."

Miss Evans was about to call a cease-fire when a tremendous crash rocked the whole house. Glass shattered. Beth cried out and Shannon screamed. The glow from the fireplace grew brighter as cold air blew in from the broken windows. Miss Evans remained sitting but with her head down on her chest. At first, Beth thought she'd been hurt, then she realized that the old lady was praying.

Virginia rushed back into the parlor with the lantern. She held the lamp tightly. Branches of a tree were poking through the broken windows, and when Virginia opened the front door she faced a wall of tree limbs. What was left of the porch roof lay underneath the fallen tree, and Virginia could see that a portion of Beth's room was also damaged.

"That big oak—" Virginia stammered.

"Hit by lightning, more than likely," Miss Evans concluded, standing behind her. "Another ten feet this way and it would have landed in our laps."

She took the lamp from Mrs. Cooper's shaking hands. "There's nothing we can do tonight. We'll just pray that it won't rain hard enough to leak in on the floors. You two girls might as well call it a day. You can lock horns again tomorrow after church."

"Church?" Beth asked, looking at her mother.

"You do go to church around here, don't you?" Miss Evans asked.

Virginia sighed. "We haven't been lately. But, well, it wouldn't do us any harm, I guess."

"It appears to me you have some things to be thankful for," Miss Evans observed.

"But, Mom—"

"Well, *I'm* not going!" Shannon declared and headed upstairs.

"Mom," Beth whined, "I wanted to take Nutmeg out in the morning."

"Beth, please. I don't need any static from you right now. This is going to cost us a bundle to fix. I'm already over my head on this place." Mrs. Cooper turned away. "Please, dear, just go to bed."

Beth was hurt and angry. "Am I supposed to sleep in my room with the tree?"

"No, no, of course not. Crawl into my bed." Worry flattened her mother's voice.

Miss Evans had gone ahead to the dining room with the lamp. She was talking on the telephone. "That's right. That's what I said; we have a tree on the front porch. Yes, that would help. See you in the morning." She hung up. "Chuck said he'd come out with his chain saw after church tomorrow."

Virginia nodded gratefully. She sat at the dining room table and stared at the still unfinished new kitchen.

"Change is always hard," Miss Evans observed. "Good night, Virginia." She laid a wrinkled hand on the younger woman's head and went up the dining room stairs.

Beth found her mother sitting in the dark with her head down on her arms. "I came to say good-night," she said.

Virginia reached out to the girl. "I wonder if we're doing the right thing, Beth. Maybe we've bitten off more than we can chew."

For a moment Beth was at a loss for words. Then she ran her hand down her mother's silky black hair. "Daddy told me once that quitters *never* win."

The church in Cooper's Creek was a surprise to both Beth and her mother. Virginia felt a sense of peace in the little sanctuary. She realized that she'd missed attending church in the years since her husband's death. Beth had expected to be bored but found herself listening to Chuck Warren in the pulpit. The young preacher made the Bible lesson interesting, like it mattered somehow. He talked about not being afraid. He told the congregation that God was everywhere. He read from the Psalms.

"If I ascend up into heaven, thou art there; if I make my bed in hell, behold, thou art there. If I take the wings of the morning, and dwell in the uttermost parts of the sea, even there shall thy hand lead me and thy right hand shall hold me. If I say, Surely the darkness shall cover me; even the night shall be light about me. Yea, darkness hideth not from thee, but the night shineth as the day; the darkness and the light are both alike to thee."

Beth liked those verses. It almost sounded like a song. She tried to make up a tune for it on the way home.

Chuck Warren drove out right behind them to remove the tree and board up the broken windows. Virginia figured the least she could do was invite the man to dinner too. Fortunately, the electricity had come back on in the night and her new stove was installed.

"This isn't much of a Sabbath rest for you, is it?" she said when she called him to the table. He turned off the chain saw and shrugged. The rain had turned to snow in the night and Chuck was standing in muddy slush now.

After dinner, Virginia tried to write him a check.

"Oh, no," he said. "This is the Lord's day. True worship, you know, is taking care of widows and orphans." He waved the check aside. "No, this job is a gift."

Virginia stammered her thanks. Then Chuck's smile faded a bit.

"There is one thing you can do, though," he said. "Call Sheriff Larsen and have him come out tomorrow. I want him to take a look at something."

Virginia caught the concern in his voice. "What—?"

Chuck stood looking at the mess outside the front door. "That tree wasn't hit by lightning, Mrs. Cooper. It was axed half through. The wind did the rest."

CHAPTER 5

Chuck had most of the tree cleared away by the next afternoon. Mrs. Cooper stared at the damage to the house and hardly noticed Sheriff Larsen's arrival. Chuck showed him the stump of the tree and the chips of wood at its base that had made him suspicious.

Paul pushed his hat back on his head. "I just can't figure out why anyone would do something like this," he admitted. "People in these parts might be standoffish, but they're not vicious."

Virginia sat on the new tree stump and picked at the bark. She looked tired.

"You mind if I do some looking around down the lane?" the sheriff asked her. "There are a couple of abandoned mines down toward the lake that I'd like to check out."

"Help yourself," Virginia said and walked off. She stood looking again at the house. Chuck came up behind her.

"What will it cost to have all that fixed?" she asked dully.

"Oh, not much—we can have it—"

"Don't give me that 'not much' business," Virginia protested sharply. "I'm not that stupid, and I'm not on welfare yet either. You charge me what you charge everybody else. The Sabbath ended yesterday at sundown."

Sheriff Larsen drove the jeep far down the rutted lane toward the lake. At the crash site he stopped and spent several minutes walking around the wreckage again. The lack of suitcases in the wreckage troubled him. The fire and explosion had destroyed nearly everything, but Paul and his men had gone over the charred remains carefully, looking for clues to the dead men's identities. They had found one suitcase, nothing else. No guns for hunting, no fishing reels.

He stood again now, feeling strongly that there were more people involved. He was sorry that the rain and storms of the past weeks had washed away all other signs.

There must have been something else in that plane, reasoned the man to himself. *A cargo; maybe an illegal one.* That would explain why the plane had been flying so low as it neared the international border. *And if I'm right, then the cargo could still be around here someplace.*

He returned to his vehicle and continued

toward the lake. He parked off the lane in a clump
of trees and continued on foot down a cowpath
that was nearly overgrown from lack of use.

The mouth of a mine stood gaping from the
side of the gully ahead of him. A skull and cross-
bones crudely painted on a board warned of poisonous gas within. Paul lit the lantern he'd
brought from the car—standard equipment in
mine country—and entered the cold, dark mine
shaft. A flashlight would have given more light but
would not have warned of decreasing oxygen as
the lantern's flame would do.

At a Y in the shaft, another warning sign was
posted. Paul decided to search the left branch first.
He started to turn when he heard a stone scrape
behind him.

A sharp blow on the head tumbled the sheriff to
the ground. A tall, dark-clothed figure behind the
fallen man struck a match. The burst of flame illu-
minated his chiseled face as he lit a cigarette.
Beneath a thin moustache, his lips curled into a
cruel smile. He threw the match onto the ground
beside the fallen man and walked away.

Later that day, a flashy red sports car pulled to
a stop at Cooper's house. A tall, well-dressed man
came to the living room door. He bowed when Virginia answered his knock.

"I would have come to your front door,
madame, but it was impossible—" His accent was
pleasantly French.

Virginia blushed and pushed a lock of hair
back in place. She'd been folding laundry in the
living room. "I know; I'm sorry. We had a bit of an

accident." She hid the underwear under a towel.

"Nothing serious, I trust," the man touched the tips of his thin moustache. "I have come about a room," he added. "This is the boarding house I read about in the paper?"

"Why, yes, we are—I mean, it is," Virginia stammered. "As a matter of fact, I have another room ready." She beckoned him to follow as she headed for the front stairs. "We're renovating. We just moved in a short while ago ourselves and I only have three bedrooms ready to use. Two of them are already taken. Here, my daughter calls this the 'autumn room.' "

The third bedroom upstairs was done in browns, rust and golds. It looked like a man's room and Virginia was pleased to show it to the gentleman.

"Splendid!" he declared. "I'll take it!" He tossed his driving gloves on the bed. "I am Jacques Gautier, madame, and you must be Mrs. Cooper. I am a photographer," he went on. "I work for *Les Maisons Belles*, a periodical in Montreal. I have been traveling in your West and am looking for houses to use in feature articles."

Virginia beamed. "How very nice! I hope you'll find something of interest in this area." She took leave of her new boarder and hurried to the nearly finished new kitchen. Miss Evans was sitting on a stool, munching on an apple while she peeled potatoes. The older woman seemed to enjoy cooking and Virginia was happy to let her do it.

"What are we having tonight?" Virginia asked.

"Hash," Miss Evans reminded her.

"Oh, dear," Virginia muttered. "We'd better

change that." She opened the freezer. "Here, thaw out these steaks in the microwave. We have another guest at table tonight."

Miss Evans raised her eyebrows. "A man, I'll bet."

After the dinner was over, Mr. Gautier asked to walk with Mrs. Cooper down the lane. When her mother accepted the invitation, Beth almost choked on a mouthful of potatoes. She had already nicknamed their new guest "old snake eyes."

Mr. Gautier asked Virginia many questions as they walked slowly down the lane. "I am interested in this area," he explained. "And your neighbors, what about them?" he probed.

Virginia was perplexed at this line of questions. She shrugged. "I don't know any of them, really," she confessed. Then she added, "I understand there's a man and his son living farther down our road and there's a couple of families back up on the lake road. Why?"

"Oh, history, local flavor. It all adds to the spirit of the place."

They came to the site of the plane wreck. "What happened here?" Gautier asked.

Virginia shivered. "Some hunters crashed in a storm. At least that's the official report."

"What do you mean, official report? Is there another theory?"

Jacques's eyes no longer seemed friendly, but veiled. Virginia suddenly felt very cold.

"I need to get back to the house now," she said tersely.

"Of course," Jacques's tone changed. "I'm

sorry. It must be distressing to have death come so close to your home."

Vince Daggett had been watching the Cooper house when Gautier and the woman set out on their walk. Something about the tall man looked familiar to him. He followed them, keeping hidden. At the site of the plane wreck he watched the man smoke a cigarette. That's when he remembered where he'd seen the man before—right there, at the crash site, with another, smaller man. Vince broke out in a cold sweat despite the chilly evening air. Things were moving too fast.

Daggett had begun to feel pressure days ago when Osborne had introduced him to their third partner, the deputy sheriff, Moran.

"He gets a piece of the action for ignoring my little operation up in Marble City," Osborne had explained. "He's been around awhile—has contacts in Las Vegas. I thought he might be of help to us, for a price."

Moran looked Vince over with open disgust. "Where is the coke? I've got to know what quality it is if I'm going to sell it." The man's tone made Vince nervous. The man himself made Vince nervous. A crooked cop could play on either side.

"A third—no more—for you both," Vince had conceded. "And I'll get you some to sample, but I ain't telling you where it is!"

Osborne and Moran had exchanged meaningful glances before they left and Vince had been uneasy about the hiding place ever since. Now the scheme was further complicated by the Frenchman actually staying in the house. Vince was nearly sick at the thought.

When he returned home, he found Joey playing the piano again. "Stop that racket!" he shouted. Furball took his position beside the boy, his lips curled back from his teeth.

"I want you to go back in there tonight and check our stuff," Vince ordered. "Bring a sack out with you." He paced back and forth across the living room. "Wait 'til after midnight." He went to the kitchen for a beer and slumped down in front of the television.

Joey looked perplexed. "Dad, it's not easy for me to go back in there now. There's more people there now. I can't help making noise—"

Vince's eyes blazed. "Don't argue! Don't you think I know?"

Joey looked at his father as though he were seeing an unpleasant stranger for the first time. Revulsion and pity churned within him.

"Okay, Dad," he said. "I'll go."

The nights were getting steadily colder. At midnight Joey put on his coat and called Furball to him.

"The dog stays here," Vince mumbled from the couch. Joey had thought his father was asleep. He started to protest.

"No sass," Vince silenced him. "It's too risky as it is. You go. I'll take care of the dog. He'll be alright." He jerked the dog's collar roughly as Furball tried to follow Joey. "You git now!" Vince ordered.

Joey left Furball uneasily. But as he neared the Cooper's house, his fear of being discovered overrode all other fears. Nutmeg stirred when Joey entered the barn. The boy quickly ducked into the tack room and opened the hatch. The darkness of the tunnel was like a tomb. He stood in the middle of the darkness and felt the silence. The darkness and the emptiness were also within him. He felt a sudden pang of concern for Furball and pushed it aside. Then he concentrated on his mission. The next stage of the trip needed all his attention.

The broken-down stairs in the woodshed that went up to the little room was the most exposed part of the route. If Joey was going to be heard and discovered by someone in the house, it would happen there. He took a deep breath, then nimbly climbed the steps, stretching past the board that always squeaked.

In moments he was through the tiny room and in the crawl space. Everything was as he'd left it. "I wish Dad didn't know about this place," he murmured. He tucked one sack of the white powder under his sweater and tucked his sweater into his pants.

He inched out of the crawl space backwards and replaced the false back of the cupboard that hid its entrance. He had just stepped out onto the top stair to the woodshed when he heard footsteps. Someone came to the door connecting the old kitchen to the woodshed and opened it. Joey froze in place. His only hope of remaining unseen was that the shed was unlit. He saw Mrs. Cooper clutch her bathrobe tighter as she went for more firewood. After she loaded her arms she went back into the house.

Joey shivered, more from fear than from the

cold. He heard Mrs. Cooper add more fuel to the wood-burning stove. He didn't dare climb down the broken stairs. After what seemed like an hour, he moved back into the tiny room. His legs were cramping and he sat on the floor and rubbed them.

Time crawled by and the icy air penetrated to Joey's bones. When the house seemed quiet, he tried the stairs again and made it safely. It was hard to be quiet when his body was clumsy with cold. He was still shaking with fear as he jogged through the tunnel.

When he arrived back at his house neither Vince nor Furball was there. The blackness of the tunnel seemed to surround him once more. A sick feeling crept around his stomach. He put the sack of cocaine on the kitchen table and looked back in his room for his dog. Then he heard his dad come in and go to the kitchen sink to wash his hands.

Joey stood by the door and watched him. "Where's Furball?" he asked.

Vince ignored him. He picked up the sack of the narcotic and shoved it inside his coat.

"Dad, where's Furball? I can't find him." Joey's voice quivered.

Vince headed for the front door and shoved Joey aside. Joey clutched at his father's coat. "Dad,—my dog?" he begged, stumbling along beside him.

Vince pushed the boy away. Joey fell out through the door and against the porch railing. It broke beneath the sudden weight.

"I had enough of that animal snarling and snapping at me every time I come into my own house!" Vince growled. He strode toward his truck.

Joey staggered to his feet and went after him. "If you treated him nice once in awhile, he'd—"

Vince faced the boy. "Stop snivelling! There's only one way to train animals. You show 'em who's boss. That dog of yours was half wolf, half wild. You couldn't teach him nuthin'!"

Vince looked away as though he couldn't meet his son's eyes. He cursed and spat. "He was just a dumb animal," he snapped. He turned away and got into his truck. "Now quit acting like a baby and git back in the house. I gotta take this stuff to Moran." He started the ignition.

Joey felt bile rising in his throat. Grief and hatred rose like fire and blinded him.

"My dog!" he screamed. "You killed my dog!" He rushed at the truck and struck the window next to his father. He heard it shatter under his blow but felt no pain as the glass cut into his hand.

Vince stomped on the gas pedal and spun away, leaving Joey stumbling in the road. The boy fell to his knees, choking on his cries.

"Time he growed up," Vince said to himself as he drove off.

CHAPTER 6

It had been more than a week since Joey told Beth about his snake. She wasn't certain she believed Joey's story about Herman, but she took a long stick with her anyway when she went to explore the chamber room after school the next day. Mrs. Cooper was using the room as a catchall for boxes and odds and ends that she had no other place to store. The chamber was even more cluttered than it had been that first day Beth explored it.

She left the door open to the hall, just in case she had to make a fast exit.

"Herman," she sang out softly. "Oh, Hermy, where are you?" She stuck her stick under boxes and crates as she moved along. "I'm not going to hurt you. I'm Joey's friend." Seeing was difficult in the murky light.

Beth was checking behind an old trunk when Shannon looked in. All Shannon could see of the younger girl was her rear end poking out from behind the boxes.

"Come to Bethy, little snake," Beth sang sweetly. "Come out, come out, wherever you are."

Shannon saw a garden hose coiled near the door and held her breath to keep from making any noise. She picked it up and uncoiled a length. Then she crouched behind a stack of boxes and slowly inched her way closer to Beth's position. Her unwieldy shape made moving difficult. When she was as close as she dared get, Shannon put the hose down and began pushing it along the floor toward Beth's legs.

"Oh, Hermy, where are you?" Beth kept coaxing. She heard a soft "hssss" and looked down.

"Akkkk!!!" she screamed. "Ahhh!!" She bumped into the trunk and scrambled over it backwards, never taking her eyes off the slithering green shape behind the boxes.

She was about to bolt for the door when she saw Shannon sitting on the floor with the rest of the garden hose. The older girl was laughing so hard that tears rolled down her cheeks.

Beth flew at her and started hitting her.

"Hey, watch out! Beth, you're hurting me!" Shannon cried as she grabbed for Beth's wrists and tried to hold the enraged girl away.

"You creep!" Beth shouted. "You mean, ugly, stupid creep! I hate you!"

Miss Evans heard the ruckus from her room.

"Girls!" she admonished as she hurried to separate them. "Beth, stop this!" She pulled Beth away and shook the skinny little girl hard. "Beth Cooper, control yourself!"

Beth stood quivering, crying.

"What's going on here?" Miss Evans demanded.

"She—she scared me—" Beth's voice shook.

Shannon trembled with her own anger. "She acts like such a jerk! Sure, I played a little trick on her and she couldn't take it." She paused to catch her breath. "So she tries to beat me up like I was some stupid kid. I'm going to have a baby!" she shouted at Beth. "Can't you see that?"

"Well, why don't you act like it then?!" Beth yelled back and then ran from the room.

Shannon dusted off her slacks. "I really didn't need any help. I'm quite capable of taking care of myself." She walked away, leaving Miss Evans alone in the dark room.

"Yes, I can see that," she murmured facetiously.

Beth kept running all the way to the barn. She climbed on a hay bale and threw the saddle on Nutmeg's back.

"It's enough to make you sick," she complained to the horse. She jabbed the mare in the belly to make her exhale the air she was holding then cinched the girth up another two notches. Beth wiped her eyes on her jacket sleeve.

"She just looks for ways to be mean," she went on. "And when she isn't being nasty, she's moping around the house like she was dying. Nothing is ever her fault."

Beth kept muttering as she mounted the horse and rode down the lane. The last snow had not completely melted. It lay in patches on the ground and in small drifts near the trees. Beth's breath looked like smoke in the cold air.

She drew Nutmeg up sharply when she saw someone down by the creek. As she drew closer, she recognized the sheepskin coat.

"Hey, Joey!" she shouted and reined the horse in his direction. Joey's eyes looked red and puffy. He stuck his hands in his pockets. One of them was bandaged. "Whatcha doing?" Beth asked.

"Nuthin'."

"How come I didn't see you after school?" Then, without waiting for an answer, "Where's Furball?" Beth asked, looking around.

Joey made a kind of choking sound. He wouldn't look at the girl. "He's dead."

"Oh, Joey, you're kidding! Oh, no!" Beth slid off Nutmeg's back, her own troubles forgotten. "Was he hit by a car or something?"

"Yeah—yeah, it was an accident, I guess."

Beth stood beside the boy. "I'm awfully sorry, Joey. I . . ."

Joey looked at the skinny little redhead. "You been cryin' too?"

Beth nodded, looking at the ground. "I'm going down to the lake. I thought I'd run away."

"Run away?" Joey asked as he stroked Nutmeg's head sadly.

"Just for today—everybody at my house is weird."

Joey put his hands on his hips. "Running away won't help."

"Ah, I'll go back," she conceded. "But not 'til I'm ready. You want to come with me?"

Joey shrugged. "How am I supposed to do that when you've only got one horse?"

Beth knit her eyebrows together and looked at Nutmeg's back. "We could both fit, couldn't we?" Joey gave one of her curls a yank and smiled despite the heaviness in his chest. "Yeah, Red, I guess we could."

Once they were on board, Beth gave Nutmeg a kick in the side. "You'd better be nice to me or I'll make her run and then you'll be sorry!" Beth's laugh was infectious and Joey smiled in spite of himself.

They were nearing the lake when Joey suddenly reached for the reins. Beth was right in the middle of singing "Home on the Range."

"Look!" he said and pointed to a clump of trees. They slid off the horse and went to investigate. The sheriff's jeep was parked there. Two tires were slashed and the radio was torn out.

Joey grew pale. "Stay here!" he ordered. He began circling around the vehicle, fearing what he would find.

"Who does he think he is, ordering me around?" Beth complained as she tied Nutmeg to a tree. She headed down an overgrown path that ended at a gully. Beth spotted the abandoned mine workings.

"Hot diggity!" she exclaimed. She ran to the mouth of the mine and only glanced at the warning sign at the entrance. She walked slowly into the darkness, sniffing the air, wondering what poisonous fumes smelled like. The gloom of the mine and the second warning sign at the Y dampened her curiosity. As she turned to go back, she glimpsed a man's boots. Her eyes bugged open. Inching toward the boots, she made out the body lying on the ground. The shock of it seemed to hit her like a blow.

"Joey!" she screamed as she ran for the sunlight. "Joey!" She nearly knocked the boy down as she ran up the path. "Joey, there's a man in there! In the mine!" She pointed. "I think he's dead!"

Joey grabbed her shoulders and held her. A look of sick terror crossed his face. Then he ran toward the mine. "Now, stay outside!" he yelled back at her. This time she obeyed.

Joey quickly found the sheriff and felt his neck for a pulse. "He's alive!" he sobbed. He scrambled to his feet and ran back to Beth.

"We've got to get help—fast! It's the sheriff. Get on your horse and call an ambulance! I'll stay here."

Beth started running, then stopped short. "I can't get on her without something to stand on!" she wailed.

Joey shook his head and ran after her. He heaved her up onto the saddle and handed her the reins. Their eyes met just for a second. The sadness in his eyes stabbed her.

"Get going!" Joey commanded, whacking the horse's rump. "Run hard!"

Beth held on as Nutmeg bolted and stretched out into a hard run. Beth could hardly see. Tears streamed down her cheeks as the cold air whipped across her face. She felt like she was flying.

"Come on, girl!" she urged. "Faster! Faster!"

The thought of stopping didn't cross Beth's mind until they raced past the house. She hauled back on the reins. Nutmeg fought for her head and broke stride. Beth fought the horse and ended up falling out of the saddle in the front yard. Her breath was knocked out of her. She rolled over and tried to stand up.

"Mom!" she gasped. "Mom! Call an ambulance!"

Shannon came out the side door and headed up the road to get the horse. "You weren't hurt that bad, you turkey!" she said.

"No!" Beth protested. "You don't understand!" She limped to the south porch. "Mom!" she yelled. "Call an ambulance! The sheriff—he's hurt bad—down in the mine."

Mrs. Cooper jumped for the telephone to make the call. Mr. Gautier stood by, watching. "How unfortunate!" he observed. "Does she often play down in the gully?"

"The gully?" Virginia asked. "What gully?"

Mr. Gautier responded quickly. "Oh, I thought she said something about a gully."

By the time the ambulance arrived Mrs. Cooper had the car ready so that Beth could lead them down to the mine. Beth hung out the car window to wave them on. Shannon was in the barn rubbing down the sweating horse. The deputy sheriff's car followed the ambulance.

All of the vehicles parked near the sheriff's jeep. Beth led the two paramedics, her mother and the deputy sheriff down the cow path. Deputy Moran motioned the others to stay outside, then led the paramedics into the mine shaft.

Joey was sitting, shivering, beside the unconscious man, rubbing the sheriff's frostbitten hands. He had taken off his coat and sweater to cover the sheriff's body.

"We wondered why he didn't check in this morning," Moran said as he knelt beside his boss.

He took Joey aside while the medics loaded the sheriff onto the stretcher. "You're Vince Daggett's boy, aren't you?"

Joey nodded. "Yessir. Can't we go outside? I'm freezing."

"Sure, in a minute. What were you doing around here?"

"I came with Beth. We were just riding her horse and we saw the jeep. I figured the sheriff had to be around here somewhere."

"You know what he was looking for in this mine?"

Joey was glad the mine was dark. "No, sir."

Moran looked intently at the boy and laughed softly. "That's right, kid. You don't know anything about anything." He directed his flashlight's beam along the walls of the mine shaft. "This isn't all that good a hiding place anyway, is it?"

Joey didn't answer, and the deputy left the confused boy standing in the mine alone. When Joey came out of the mine he was surprised to see Beth and Mrs. Cooper waiting for him. Beth handed him his coat and sweater. "You've got blue lips," she said.

Mrs. Cooper led them to her car. "Get in. I'm taking you both home for something warm. Deputy Moran will be back to talk with you."

"Moran?" Joey asked. "You said 'Deputy Moran'?"

"Yeah," Beth answered. "You know him?"

"No, no—my dad does, I guess. I've heard his name is all." Joey was silent all the way up the lane.

At the house Virginia put hot apple pie in front of both the youngsters. Joey was on his third helping when the deputy returned.

"How is the sheriff?" Mrs. Cooper asked.

Moran took out a small notebook and a pen. "He has a concussion; he'll be laid up for awhile." He looked at Mrs. Cooper warmly. "I'll be in charge of the investigation 'til he's back," he said with a smile.

Virginia looked away.

"You mean you're going to find out who clobbered him?" Beth asked.

Moran ignored her question. "I need statements from you two," he said, looking at Joey.

Joey wouldn't look at the deputy. "I already told you everything I know. I don't know any more." He seemed sullen. "Can I go now?"

"You don't think this is connected with the plane that crashed, do you?" Moran asked pointedly.

Beth and her mother both looked confused by his question. Joey stood absolutely still. "With the plane, sir? Why, no."

Moran gave Joey a look that made Beth shiver. "Okay, kid, go ahead. Give my regards to your pa."

Beth walked with Joey to the door. She watched as he ran into the woods. "Everybody's weird," she decided.

Beth didn't see Joey at school again the next

day. When she got home the house seemed empty. A note from her mother explained that she had taken Shannon to Coeur d'Alene for a doctor's appointment. "Old snake eyes" was gone also, which suited Beth just fine.

She hunted around the kitchen until she found the leftover pie in the pots and pans drawer. She took a fat slice and wandered out to the barn. Nutmeg obliged her by licking her fingers clean.

Beth got the currycomb and began working on the horse's coat. "I wish Mr. Larsen would get better quick so he could give me some more lessons," she told Nutmeg. The horse just looked at her with big, liquid brown eyes. "I'm glad we found him." Her thoughts were interrupted by a scuffing noise from the tack room.

"Joey?" Beth called. "Joey, is that you? I missed you at school." The tack room smelled of old leather. Beth could see part of a harness hanging from a wooden peg on the wall. A few bales of hay lay strewn about. She was about to call again when she stubbed her toe on something on the floor. When she looked down, she saw a ring set into the wood.

For a moment she forgot about the noise. She knelt down and pulled up on the ring. A trapdoor lifted.

"Oh, man!" she exclaimed. She was peering down into the blackness when a big fleshy hand pushed her from behind. She hit her head as she fell into the hole. The heavy trapdoor slammed shut above her.

Mr. Osborne stood on the door and wrung his hands. "Oh me! Complications!" he said, wiping his forehead. He went to the bales of hay he'd been hiding behind and pulled them over the trapdoor to keep it shut. As he retreated from the tack room, he nearly ran into the tall, dark man who stood watching him.

"Ohhh!" Mr. Osborne jumped.

"Pleasant day, wouldn't you say?" Mr. Gautier asked.

"Yes, yes, very nice—nice d—d—day," the chubby realtor stammered. He cleared his throat.

"And who might you be?" the Frenchman asked.

"Ah—ah—Osborne's the name. Fred Osborne, realtor. I'm—I'm here on b—I came to, ah, speak with Mrs. Cooper—about selling." His smile locked into place at last.

"And you're looking for her in the barn," Gautier stated.

"Ah, yes,—well, no—no, I, ah, needed to, ah, I had to check out the condition—you know, of the property."

Gautier took a razor-sharp stiletto from a sheath under his arm and began playing with the deadly-looking knife.

Osborne paled noticeably. "My client needed to know about the barn," he said and gulped.

Gautier began cleaning under his fingernails with the weapon. "And you found what you were looking for?"

"No! Oh, no! No, I didn't," Osborne blurted out. "I mean, well, not really. But then I guess I don't need to know everything, do I?"

"What do you know?" Gautier asked, holding the stiletto very still.

"Only that—that this is very valuable p—p—property, yes, indeed, very va—valuable property—land." Osborne almost cried for joy when he saw Miss Evans come into the barn.

"There you are, Mr. Gautier!" she said. "There's some fellow on the phone for you—sounds real important." She looked from one man to the other. "I didn't mean to interrupt."

"No, no problem," Mr. Osborne said. "I was—was just leaving." He put on his hat. "Ah, just tell Mrs. Cooper that, ah, Fred Osborne was here. If she should change her mind about selling . . ."

He tipped his hat to the old woman and hurried away. Mr. Gautier had slipped the knife back into its sheath when Miss Evans first spoke. As Osborne hastened out to the road, Gautier scowled after him and then walked brusquely to the house.

Mr. Osborne nearly ruined his car getting back to town. He was still shaking and his face was a sickly gray pallor when he parked in front of his office. He locked the door of the office and sagged against it.

"I can't take this," he gasped, loosening his tie. He reached into his desk drawer for his bottle of whiskey and drank some down right from the bottle. Then he reached for the telephone. His hands shook.

"Northwest Travel? Yes, Fred Osborne here. Have you got anything leaving for Mexico soon? Yes,—tonight? Yes, yes, I'll take it. I'll pick up the tickets in about an hour."

His second call was to the sheriff's department. He left word for Deputy Moran to come by his office as soon as possible. Then he went upstairs to his bachelor's apartment and began packing.

When Moran arrived, Osborne was loading his suitcases into his car. "That French guy out there at Cooper's—he's on to us. He caught me looking through the barn—I was just checking around like you told me to," he sputtered.

Moran chuckled. "And you panicked? I always said you ought to stick to the small rackets." He leaned on Osborne's car. "So you're leaving? What about your percentage?"

"Dead men don't collect percentages!" Osborne slammed the lid of the car trunk shut. "You and Daggett will be lucky if you just end up in jail!"

"With me handling the investigation? Small chance. With any luck at all, we'll be counting our money by the time the sheriff gets out of the hospital."

Osborne started his car. "Do me a favor and forget I ever got you together with Daggett," he begged. He gunned the engine and left Cooper's Creek as fast as he could go.

Moran smiled as he watched the realtor drive out of sight. "My cut is getting bigger all the time."

CHAPTER 7

Beth lay in a heap in the darkness of the tunnel. The knock on her head had stunned her momentarily. She stood up slowly and tried to reach the door over her head.

"Hey!" she cried. "Hey, let me out!" She felt a ladder attached to the dirt wall and climbed it. "Let me out!" she yelled as she beat on the wooden door over her head. "Joey, if that's you, this is a crummy joke!" Her pounding only resulted in dust falling into her eyes.

The darkness of the tunnel was absolute. She held a hand in front of her face, but could not see it. Whether her eyes were open or closed, everything looked the same—black.

"Mom," she whimpered. "Mommy! Somebody

help me!" She tried again to push the door open, but it did not budge.

She struggled with the door until her arms ached. Her screams for help became only short, hoarse, choking sounds. She sat huddled on the dirt floor and sobbed. "Where am I?" she wailed. "In a well?" A hundred fears raced through her mind, each one worse than the one before.

"Oh, God," she sobbed. "Oh, God, help me!" She laid her head down on her knees and cried until she had no more tears. Her despair was interrupted by a strange thought. She remembered singing a funny song in the car—on the way home from church one day. What was it? How did it go?

Slowly the tune and the words came back to her. "If I say, Surely the darkness will cover me, even the night shall be light around me. Darkness hideth not from thee."

"Oh, yes," Beth said aloud between gasping sobs. "The night shines like the day—Oh, God," she cried, "you're here!" Her fear subsided a little and she stood up.

"I've got to get out of here," she sniffled. "Nobody'll ever find me in this hole."

She climbed the ladder and tried the door again. *That's no use,* she decided, wiping her eyes.

She slapped her hands together in the utter darkness and checked to see if her eyes were really open. They were.

"Okay, now what? Ahead, I guess." The sound of her own voice was comforting somehow. She began to feel her way along the dirt wall. "I hope there aren't any snakes in here."

The dirt under her hands was cold. She shivered and stopped. She looked back toward the ladder under the trap door. She couldn't see it. She seemed adrift in a sea of blackness.

"The Lord is my shepherd. I shall not want," she whispered, trying hard to be brave. "He leadeth me in the paths of righteousness for His name's sake . . ." Step by step she advanced, pushing aside her fear as she penetrated the darkness around her. "Surely goodness and mercy shall follow me all the days of my life," her foot suddenly touched something in front of her. She drew back, terrified.

Slowly she reached out her hand. Nothing. Then she touched a piece of wood. She felt it carefully. It was another ladder. Beth gasped and climbed it quickly. Her head bumped another wooden door above her. She prayed as she tried to push it open.

It moved. She could hardly believe it. She sobbed in relief. She saw the piles of chopped wood stacked around the trapdoor and a dim light behind it. She scampered toward the light and was amazed to discover that she was in the woodshed of her house.

When Beth bounded into the dining room she saw her mother at the telephone. Beth nearly tackled her, crying so hard that Mrs. Cooper couldn't understand what she was saying. Miss Evans and Mr. Gautier stood watching.

"Stop it, Beth," her mother said, shaking the girl gently. "Where were you? We looked everywhere. You didn't leave a note. Beth!" She held the girl in a tight embrace. "I was so afraid—after what happened to Paul."

Beth took the hanky Miss Evans held for her and blew her nose. "I was in a tunnel—I was in the barn with Nutmeg and—I heard a noise. There is this trapdoor and somebody pushed me. I couldn't get out!" She had to stop talking to keep from crying again. "It was dark; I couldn't even see my hands as I went along. There's a tunnel, Mom, underground! It comes out in the woodshed. Come on! I'll show you!"

They all followed as Beth led the way to the woodshed. The girl crouched down and led them back around the pile of wood hiding the trapdoor. Mr. Gautier whistled softly.

"See?" Beth pointed. "There's a ladder in there. Come on." She climbed back down into the hole, made braver by the light from the flashlight her mother held. Beth led her mom through the long tunnel to the other end. There she climbed the ladder and tried once again to push the door open.

"Of all the dirty tricks . . ." Mrs. Cooper muttered as she watched her daughter struggle with the door. She led Beth back to the woodshed.

Mr. Gautier accompanied them to the barn and led them into the tack room. Two heavy bales of hay lay across the trapdoor.

"Who in the world would do such a thing to a child?" Mrs. Cooper asked. "And why?" She looked at Mr. Gautier for some help in finding the answers. He stood silent, his face carefully masked from any show of thought.

Virginia pulled Beth close. "I'm going to call

that deputy sheriff. This has gone far enough."

Beth lagged behind as Mr. Gautier and her mother headed back to the house. She stayed behind to pet Nutmeg. Then she saw something move just outside the circle of light from the barn. She went toward it to see what it was. Suddenly she screamed.

Mrs. Cooper turned with a groan and ran back to the barn. "What now?"

Beth pointed to the heap of fur that moved just outside the barn door. The animal tried to snarl as they neared it, but couldn't find the strength.

"It's Furball!" Beth gasped. "Oh, Furball! Mom, it's Joey's dog!"

Mr. Gautier took one look at the injured animal. "This dog should be shot," he said. "We ought to put it out of its misery." He turned to go back toward the house. "I have a gun in my car."

"No!" Beth screamed, stopping him. She knelt beside the animal and Furball tried to lick her hand. Beth could see the path the dog had made, dragging itself through the dirty snow.

"Oh, baby, it's almost dead!" Mrs. Cooper pleaded.

"You can't kill him, you can't! He's Joey's dog! We've got to save him!" She held the dog's head in her lap and looked up at her mother.

"Oh, please," she sobbed. "We've got to try."

Mrs. Cooper smiled grimly. "Okay, we'll try, for what trying's worth." She hurried from the barn. Mr. Gautier turned to leave.

"You're wasting your time," he declared in disgust.

Furball seemed to relax as Beth petted his matted fur. All the tension and fear from her afternoon in the tunnel spilled out in her tears.

Mrs. Cooper returned with a sheet and Beth helped her wrap the dog in it. She sat in the back seat of the car with Furball on her lap as her mother drove to Coeur d'Alene to the veterinarian.

"Surely you want me to put him to sleep," the vet said after they had laid the dog on the examination table. "His injuries are extensive, internal."

Beth's face was white. "Doctor, this is a special dog. He's real valuable—my friend Joey loves him."

The vet looked at Beth and spoke softly. "I may not be able to save him. You've got to realize that before I start. Trying isn't any guarantee of success. I'm not God."

Beth nodded. "I know. But if you don't try, you don't give God a chance."

The vet took a deep breath and nodded to his assistant. "Let's go," he ordered.

Weariness enveloped the Coopers as they left the vet's office.

"Hungry?" Virginia asked.

Beth shook her head.

"How about a visit to the hospital?"

Beth looked puzzled.

"Sheriff Larsen is still there."

They arrived at the hospital just as visiting hours were ending. Mrs. Cooper hurried back to his room while Beth sank wearily on one of the couches in the lobby. Paul and Virginia walked out to the lobby so Beth could join in the visit, but the girl was fast asleep. Paul's head was still bandaged, but he looked fit. He sat near Virginia with his arm around the back of the couch behind her.

Virginia told him about the events of the day. "Mr. Osborne warned me that life was rough up here," she concluded. "But I never anticipated all this."

Paul touched his head carefully. "I'll be out of here Saturday. They want me to stay in longer, but I can't see it. I don't understand why Moran isn't moving faster on this." He stood up and paced impatiently. "I'm convinced that there's something hidden in or near your house. Something from that plane."

He looked at Beth, sleeping on the couch. "You've got to be very careful. I'm afraid the people mixed up in this wouldn't hesitate to eliminate anyone who interfered." He paused. "I guess I'm proof enough of that!"

He sat beside Virginia and took her hands in his own. Her hands were white and soft against his hardened, weathered ones. "Promise me you'll be careful. And try not to judge us here by all this. That house is all you've said it was; you've made it beautiful again. I guess I misjudged it—and you."

Virginia rallied a smile in spite of her fatigue. "Thank you. I promise I'll wait and see—once this is over—if I make it 'til then."

A stout nurse approached them ominously. Paul patted Virginia's hands and tousled Beth's curls. "Good night," he said and dutifully followed the nurse back to his room.

Mr. Gautier took advantage of the Coopers'

absence. He went into Virginia's office, just off the parlor, as soon as he knew they'd left with the dog. He began tapping the walls.

Shannon heard him in there when she came to the parlor to study. "Lose something?" she asked as she looked in. Gautier gave her a cold look.

"I study old houses," he said. "It is my job."

Shannon shrugged and went back to the couch. She flipped open her algebra book. "Even school was better than living like this," she complained to Miss Evans when the older woman entered the parlor.

Miss Evans had taken to wearing a cowboy hat and boots along with her coveralls. She sat in her rocking chair and took up her knitting.

The woman's peacefulness infuriated Shannon. "Did anyone ever tell you you look like a scarecrow?" the girl asked.

Miss Evans smiled. "It's always nice to be useful," she observed.

Shannon slammed her book shut. "What's with you?" she asked. "Don't you care what people think about you?"

Miss Evans pushed her bifocals up on her nose. "Gave that up a long time ago. As long as the Lord and I are on good terms, well, I guess it's His opinion of me that matters. Besides, I can't control what you think about me." She pulled out a length of yarn from the ball on her lap. "But what I think about you, well now, that's another matter. I have some say about that."

"And just what do you think about me?" Shannon asked, feigning indifference.

Mr. Gautier walked through the room looking

at Miss Evans and Shannon. He was disgusted, as usual.

Miss Evans laid down her knitting and looked Shannon right in the eye. "I think you are an intelligent, lovely young girl. You have a lot to give to life and a lot yet to learn about life. I pray for your peace every day, and for your baby."

Shannon was uneasy under Miss Evans's gaze and with the unexpected praise. She pushed herself off the couch. "Save your prayers. I don't think God even knows I'm alive."

She lumbered upstairs and was about to enter the bathroom when she noticed that the door to the storage chamber was ajar. She walked down the hall, pushed the door open and went in.

Mr. Gautier was searching through the crates and boxes. He began searching along the wall beneath the little window at the far end when Shannon noisily cleared her throat.

Gautier looked up, startled.

"Quite an interesting house, isn't it? I'm sure Mrs. Cooper would be happy to give you a guided tour."

Gautier straightened up and glared at the pregnant girl. "You really are quite a nuisance," he said.

Miss Evans round them there, staring across the room at each other. "Either of you hear Mrs. Cooper say anything about a delivery of wood? There's a man downstairs wants to unload some in the woodshed. And at suppertime; can you imagine?"

Mr. Gautier hurried from the room, brushing

past the women as though they weren't even there. They followed him to the woodshed.

Vince Daggett stood at the back door of the old kitchen. Joey stood behind him, staring at the ground. The pickup truck was half full of wood.

"Now you hustle," Vince hissed, as he heard the people returning. "You fill that gunnysack while I unload the wood. We can't wait no longer."

Mr. Gautier looked Daggett over carefully. Vince stared back at the Frenchman.

"Go right ahead," Gautier told the woodsman. Vince nodded and moved the truck around to the back of the woodshed and opened the barn-type doors.

Gautier leaned against the door separating the woodshed from the old kitchen, right by the broken stairs that went up to the little room. He lit a cigarette and leisurely watched the unloading operation.

Joey looked at his father and helped with the wood.

"Mrs. Cooper must intend to burn a lot of wood this winter," Gautier observed. Wood already lined two walls of the shed.

Daggett shrugged. "No tellin'," he answered. "All I do is deliver where I'm asked."

When the job was half done, Daggett stopped to wipe the sweat from his brow. "You planning on standing there watching or did you want to help?"

Gautier smiled. "You know how it is. Things have a way of getting stolen if they're not looked after properly."

Vince blanched. Gautier's smile was thin. "Now

we wouldn't want anything like that to happen here, would we?"

Daggett turned quickly back to his work. Joey noticed that his father's hands were shaking.

CHAPTER 8

Pastor Warren came to Sunday dinner with Sheriff Larsen to celebrate a late Thanksgiving with the Coopers. When Beth met them at the front door, the sheriff took her hand solemnly.

"Thank you for finding me, and for riding like you did for help. The doctors think I wouldn't have lasted much longer in that cold mine."

Beth blushed. "Joey Daggett helped me. He stayed with you and covered you up with his coat."

"Too bad he's not here. I'd like to thank him too," Paul said.

Beth smiled. "He's coming over! We've got a surprise for him and he can't even start to figure out what it is!"

Joey showed up just as everyone was gathering around the table. He took his place awkwardly beside Pastor Warren. Virginia nodded to the pastor and he stood up. Miss Evans bowed her head and everyone copied her.

"Father, our hearts are filled with praise and gratitude this Thanksgiving season. We especially thank you for your love revealed in the sacrifice of your Son, Jesus Christ. And thank you for the evidences of your love in friends and homes, and in the bounty of this table. Amen."

Chuck took his seat and broke the awkward silence by grabbing the platter of meat and digging in.

Sheriff Larsen sat across the table from Mr. Gautier. "What was the name of that magazine you work for?" he asked the Frenchman as he helped himself to the steaming mashed potatoes.

"It is a small magazine," Mr. Gautier answered casually. "Not one you would know about in the States." He took a generous helping of turkey and handed it politely to Shannon.

"*Les Maisons Belles* is the name of it, didn't you say?" Virginia offered. "I haven't found it sold anywhere around here." She passed the gravy to Chuck.

"Will you come out to the barn with me later?" Beth asked the sheriff, unaware that she was changing the subject. Mr. Gautier relaxed. Beth continued. "I want to show you the tunnel I got pushed into."

Joey nearly choked on the roll he was eating. Chuck thumped him on the back.

"The craziest things have been happening

around here," Mrs. Cooper explained to Chuck. "Which reminds me, Joey, I didn't order that wood from your father . . ."

Joey looked nervous. "Oh, I—I didn't know. He must have gotten mixed up . . ."

Virginia sighed and shrugged. "Well, I suppose I'll need it this winter." Gautier was watching Joey while Virginia talked. Sheriff Larsen watched Gautier. "I guess I ought to pay for it, if I'm going to use it," Virginia went on. "Remind me to send a check home with you."

After the table had been cleared of the main meal, Miss Evans brought out a huge, flaming plum pudding and set it in the middle of the table. Ohs and ahs greeted the dramatic looking dessert.

"It isn't much, but it's my contribution to our Thanksgiving celebration, even if it is already December," she said as she sat down.

"Stella, it looks delicious. I'm going to have to hire you as cook!" Virginia exclaimed.

"Remind me not to come back," Shannon muttered beneath the chatter.

"With pleasure!" Beth retorted, trying to whisper.

After the dessert, Beth dragged the sheriff and Joey off to the barn. Mr. Gautier drove off in his sports car. Pastor Warren took his coffee and followed Shannon to the parlor.

"How are you doing?" he asked the girl as he sat on the couch.

Shannon shrugged. "Okay, I guess." She sat in Miss Evans's rocker.

"Have you decided what you're going to do with

the baby yet? Your parents asked me to help you work this out if I could," he explained.

"I don't know," Shannon answered without interest. "I never should have agreed to go through with this in the first place. An abortion would have been a whole lot easier!"

"For whom?" the pastor asked.

"What do you mean—for *me*, of course," she replied angrily.

Chuck walked to the front window. The porch outside was completely fixed. "What are your thoughts about the baby?"

"I don't think about it," Shannon said irritably. "Do you think I like having it mess up my life this way?"

"That baby didn't mess up your life, Shannon. You made the choices that brought you here. But that's all behind you. What are you going to do now?"

Shannon ignored him. She went to the piano and plunked on the keys. The sound was discordant.

"You could keep the baby," the pastor said.

"Sure, and be a mother while everybody else is having fun? No thanks. I'm not that stupid. I'd hate it!" Suddenly she hit the piano keys with her fist. "You want to know what I wish? I wish it would die! I wish it would just go away . . ." Tears rolled down her angry face.

Virginia stood at the parlor door. She hesitated to speak. "I couldn't help but hear . . ." She walked to the piano and reached for Shannon's hand.

"You really don't mean that, what you said."

"Oh yes I do!" Shannon retorted and yanked

her hand away. "How could you know how I feel?"

"Because I had two babies born dead, that's how."

Shannon wiped her eyes and looked hesitantly at Virginia.

"After the last one came—dead, my doctors told me I'd never be able to carry a baby full term. In a way, Shannon, I envy you very much." She paused and sighed. "It was hard on us. Ed, my husband, wanted a baby as much as I did. Finally we decided to find a child who needed us as much as we needed him—or her. We found Beth."

Virginia walked back to the parlor door. "I love her very, very much. And, you know, if I ever met the woman who carried her, I'd thank her. She gave Beth something I could never give any child."

Shannon waited, questioning.

"She gave her life, Shannon, life." Virginia nodded at Chuck and closed the door as she left.

At the barn, Joey stood quietly while Beth showed Sheriff Larsen the trapdoor in the tack room.

"And there's nothing in there?" the sheriff asked her.

"Nope. We took a flashlight—it's just dirt. How come it's here?"

Paul pulled a piece of hay out of a bale and chewed on it. "Well, I've heard that back east where there're blizzards, folks used to dig such tunnels so they could get to their livestock no matter what the weather was like. I suppose when your great granddaddy came out here to settle, he just naturally added this to the layout."

Beth looked disappointed. "I was hoping it was for Indians or treasure or . . ."

The sound of whining and scratching drew them into the barn. Joey reacted to the noise with a start. Beth giggled and took his hand. Then she took off her neck scarf and tied it over his eyes.

"I told you we had a surprise for you!"

She led him across the barn to the unused stall next to Nutmeg's. In the front, near the gate to the stall, Furball struggled to get out. As Joey came nearer, the dog worked harder. He had a patch over one eye, and bandages around his head and ribs.

The sheriff knelt down beside the animal and quieted him. He nodded to Beth.

She positioned Joey at the head of the stall. "Okay, guess!"

Furball barked and Joey yanked off the scarf. He stood motionless.

"Furball?" he whispered. He knelt beside the dog and stroked his fur in disbelief.

"We found him and I wouldn't let old snake eyes kill him. That's Mr. Gautier," she added for the sheriff's sake. "Mom and I took him to the vet—the dog, I mean. We just got him home yesterday. The vet said it was a miracle."

Furball started licking Joey's hand and the boy was convulsed with great aching sobs.

Beth looked at the sheriff in dismay. "I thought he'd be happy!"

Sheriff Larsen took her hand and led her away. "He is, Beth," he said. "He is."

Joey came up to the house an hour later. The

other dinner guests had already gone. Beth let Joey in at the back door.

"Thank you," he said roughly. Beth squeezed his hand and led him through the house toward the parlor.

"He can go home with you pretty soon."

"No—" Joey said quickly. "No, I don't think so. I'd like it if you—if he could stay here with you guys. I'll do chores or something to pay for his food and—and to pay for the vet."

Mrs. Cooper was sitting at the piano in the parlor, playing softly. Joey saw her there and looked away quickly.

"I've got to go home now," he stammered, inching his way toward the front door. "Ask your mom if it's okay," he said to Beth as he let himself out. The cold air came in with a gust.

"Ask me what?" Virginia asked absently as she continued playing.

Beth watched Joey hurry into the woods. "If Furball could stay here. He wants to do chores to pay for his keep," she answered.

"Another boarder, eh?" Virginia asked. "It's fine, I guess. I do need most of those logs in the woodshed split up so they'll fit in the fireplaces better."

"I wonder why he can't take him home?" Beth asked softly, still looking out the window.

Days later, the telephone on Daggett's kitchen wall rang shrilly. Joey was playing the piano and jumped to answer it. Vince grabbed the receiver out of his hands.

"Yeah," Vince answered.

"Moran," the voice announced. "I've got a buyer. Have the coke at your place day after tomorrow."

Vince breathed heavily.

"You can get it, can't you?" Moran asked.

"Yeah, sure, sure, Moran," Vince answered. "Say, I heard that Osborne left town."

"Yeah, he had business. I'm supposed to collect his cut for him."

"I'll bet you are," Vince said and hung up. Joey still stood by the piano. Vince struck the wall with his fist and cursed.

"We got to get it out, right away," he thundered.

"But how, Dad? We tried to when we took that wood over and it didn't wor—"

Vince kicked a chair out of his way. "We've gotta get it. I never should have left it there so long!"

Vince paced the floor, scratching his head. "We never shoulda put it in there in the first place. You! You're the one said it was just the spot! 'Safest place around' you said!"

Joey backed away. "It is, Dad. Nobody's found it. I didn't know the Coopers would stay. I thought Mr. Osborne was just showing the house to buyers, like he did sometimes. I didn't know the Coopers were the owners."

"Stay? Owners? You mean you knew they was around and you had me put it in there anyways?" Vince's eyes looked feverish.

"I didn't know, honest. I didn't know they'd stay!"

"And now you're over there every day, playing around, choppin' wood. I seen you. You think I don't know where you've been?"

"Dad, they're my friends." Joey went to his father and touched his arm. "Dad, do we have to go through with it? I can fix it so Beth, the girl, finds it. She'll tell the sheriff. They'll never know it was us who put it there. Nobody will. Not even that French guy. I've got it all figured out . . ."

"I bet you do!" Vince said harshly. "Well, this is one deal I'm not passing up and nobody's gonna blow it for me. You hear me? Nobody!" Vince's chest shook with an inner fury.

He opened a broom closet in the corner of the kitchen and pulled out a double-bit axe. "You like chopping wood so much," he hissed, "you chop some for me!" He thrust his axe into Joey's hands and pushed him back against the piano.

"Dad!" Joey shook his head, aghast.

Vince grabbed his arm. His fingers dug into Joey's flesh. "You been gettin' awful funny actin' since them women moved in. Piano's woman stuff, boy. Now straighten up and do's I say!"

Joey's hands seemed unable to hold up the weight of the tool.

He stared at his dad in disbelief. For a blinding, terrifying moment, Joey wanted to swing the axe around and strike his father down. The sheer power of that urge pounded against him.

"No! Oh, no!" he sobbed. He swung the axe up over his head and brought it down on the piano's keyboard. The sound was something of a death cry.

Swing after swing, Joey reduced the lovely instrument to kindling. When he could do no more he grabbed his coat and stumbled out the door.

Joey would not talk at all the next afternoon as he and Beth trudged down the dirt road from the bus stop. Beth finally gave up trying.

Beth went into her bedroom through her private door. She threw her book bag on the floor of her room and headed for the new kitchen. She stopped to pet Furball who was lying under the dining room table and then began rummaging through the kitchen cupboards for something to eat.

"There're some brownies around here somewhere," she said as she climbed up on the counter. "Aha!" she crowed as she peered into a big roasting pan on the top shelf. She broke off a hunk and jumped down. She was humming around her mouthful as she wandered out to the barn. When she pushed the door open, she was stunned to see Shannon about to get on Nutmeg's back. The horse was saddled and ready to go.

"Hey!" Beth yelled, throwing the rest of the brownie on the ground. "What do you think you're doing?"

Shannon hurried to get seated on the mare. Her pregnancy slowed her down.

"Get off her!" Beth ordered, running toward them.

Shannon jerked Nutmeg's head away from Beth's reaching hand.

"Go away!" Shannon shouted. "I'm not hurting anything! I know more about riding than you."

"Not on my horse!" Beth screamed.

Shannon headed out of the barn. Nutmeg pranced nervously.

Beth ran after the horse and rider. "You creep! Get off her! I didn't say you could ride her!" She sobbed with frustration and impotent anger, then bent to pick up several small stones. She threw them as hard as she could.

The horse pranced and shied under the barrage. One missile hit the horse hard on her neck. Nutmeg reared. Shannon was unprepared and cried out as she lost her hold. She screamed as she slid from the horse's back. Then all was silent as she lay on the snowy gravel.

Beth stood staring at the inert body in front of her. The remaining stones she was holding fell from her hand. Then Nutmeg neighed and Beth ran to catch her.

Miss Evans and Virginia had been in the fourth bedroom upstairs, looking at wallpaper samples, when the commotion in the backyard began. Virginia had gone to the window to see what it was all about. She had seen Beth throw the stones.

"Oh, no!" Virginia cried out. "Shannon's fallen off the horse!" She ran for the front stairs with Miss Evans right behind. By the time they reached Shannon, the girl was moaning softly. Virginia turned to her daughter. "You get that animal put away and get to your room. I'll deal with you later." Her tone of voice was one that Beth had never heard before. "You better pray that you haven't killed this girl's baby!"

All the blood drained from Beth's face. "But, Mom, she was on—she didn't ask—" Her words faded to silence as she watched her mother struggle to lift Shannon off the frozen ground.

"Call an ambulance!" Mrs. Cooper barked. Miss Evans rushed back into the house, her gray braids bouncing on her back.

The old woman met Beth on her way out of the dining room. "The phone is dead, Beth dear. We've got real trouble."

Beth bit her knuckles.

"You'd better go and do what your mother said. We're going to need God's help to pull out of this one!" She stopped and went back to the terrified girl and hugged her. "God's big enough to handle this," she said. "It's going to be alright."

Virginia called from her bedroom and Miss Evans hurried away. Beth dragged herself to her room and sat on the lounge chair.

"Oh, God, I didn't mean to hurt her," she sobbed. "Not that bad. Oh, please, please don't let her baby die." She couldn't go on. She curled up in a ball on the chair, paralyzed by remorse.

Miss Evans helped Virginia get Shannon on the bed. "You'll have to drive for help," Miss Evans said. "The phone's dead."

Virginia's moan was drowned beneath Shannon's cry.

"It hurts!"

"Your baby is coming," Miss Evans told her calmly. She looked at Virginia. "Before you leave, I want you to get me plenty of clean rags and set some water to boil. I've delivered plenty of babies at the mission station, and I guess I'm good for one more."

"I want a doctor!" Shannon screamed. "Don't touch me!"

Miss Evans sat down on a chair by the bed. "Suit yourself. But you're going to have a baby. If you want to do it alone, that's up to you." She turned to Virginia.

"You'd better hustle."

Virginia drove first to Daggett's house. She brought the car to a skidding stop and ran to the front door. No one answered her knock. "Oh, please," she begged, "please be home!" She tried the door and it opened.

"Hello," she shouted as she entered the front room. She was appalled at the condition of the house and noticed the remains of the piano in the corner. "Joey?"

She walked into the kitchen and saw the telephone. Her hand shook as she grabbed the receiver. "Of course it's dead," she sobbed. "We're on the same line!"

She hurried back to the car. "Oh, Joey," she whispered as she headed for town. "What's going on there?"

A few miles later she passed Mr. Gautier's red sports car on the road. She didn't even try to stop to explain what was happening at the house. He saw her barrelling down the dirt road and swerved to get well out of her way.

Just inside Cooper's Creek the speeding Audi attracted Sheriff Larsen's attention. He met Virginia at the garage as she ran to the phone booth.

"Get into my car!" he ordered when he'd heard about Shannon. He radioed for an ambulance and then turned on the siren. "Let's get back out there and see if we can help!" He reached across the seat for Virginia's hand.

"You're becoming quite adept at handling tough situations," he said tenderly. Virginia's smile was grim.

"I don't know how much more I can take."

When they turned onto the dirt road that ran past the Cooper place, they saw smoke rising above the trees.

Virginia looked at Paul and shook her head. "Oh, no," she begged. "It can't be!"

CHAPTER 9

Miss Evans sat calmly by Shannon's side. She had clean sheets and boiling water ready for the delivery.

"I want a doc—(gasp)—tor!" the girl said with clenched teeth. When the next contraction came she grabbed Miss Evans's hands and cried out.

"Why doesn't the doctor come?" Shannon asked frantically.

"It's a long way from Coeur d'Alene, dear. Nobody ever expected you to have the baby out here."

Another contraction came and gripped Shannon's body. Miss Evans held her down. "I can help you if you'll let me. I had so much training . . ." Shannon nodded from the midst of her pain.

"I was so dumb to get on that horse," she admitted as the contraction ended. "I knew it would make Beth mad."

"Watch me during this one!" Miss Evans ordered. "Breathe as I do!" She held Shannon's shoulders and kept her attention with her gaze. The old lady and the girl began breathing in rhythm.

The labor consumed all their attention. They didn't notice the spiral of smoke rising from the barn.

In her bedroom, Beth agonized through each of Shannon's cries. She stared at the closed door at the other end of the walk-through closet. "Let me help—" she whimpered as she tiptoed toward the door. As she passed the window in the closet, wisps of smoke outside caught her attention.

She ran back into her room and out onto the front porch. As she rounded the corner of the house, she saw flames filling the interior of the barn.

"Nutmeg!" she cried and ran toward the burning building.

Mr. Gautier neared the boarding house in time to see a man running away from the barn. Then he saw a stack of hay bales inside the structure burst into flame. Gautier parked his sports car on the road and ducked into the woods. He spotted Vince Daggett crouched behind a rock, watching the barn catch fire. The boy was with him. Gautier moved nearer.

Vince handed Joey a gunnysack. "Just a minute," he looked at the house, "then we go."

Just then the trio in the woods saw Beth run into the blazing barn.

Joey threw his sack down. "No! Dad, you promised nobody'd get hurt!" He started to break through the brush to run after Beth, but Vince grabbed his shoulder and held him back.

"She'll come out. You can't go—now's our chance!"

Joey struggled out of his father's grasp. Just then they heard the shriek of a siren. The sheriff's car skidded to a stop in back of the house. Paul and Virginia ran to the barn and began hosing down the outer walls. The water pressure from the garden hose was pitifully weak.

"Come on," Vince commanded. He started running toward the front door of the house.

A strained, animal cry came from behind Joey's clenched teeth. Like a cornered animal he looked around for some avenue of escape. But there was none.

"Dad!" he cried out hoarsely—and followed in his father's running steps.

Gautier watched them slip into the house, then followed carefully.

Virginia heard the horse inside the barn kicking her stall and whinnying in terror.

"The horse! We've got to get her out!" Virginia cried. She ran toward the barn, but the flames rose up to block her.

Paul pulled her back. "I'm sorry," he said. "Beth will have to get another . . ."

"Beth!" Virginia cried, then ran to the house. She burst into her bedroom and looked around frantically. Miss Evans and Shannon were going through different breathing patterns as the labor continued.

"Where's Beth?" Virginia asked.

Miss Evans looked up quickly. "I don't know. I've got my hands full here."

Shannon's face was beaded with perspiration. She cried out and reached for Miss Evans's hand again.

"The barn's on fire," Virginia told them as she hurried out. One look in Beth's bedroom told her that the girl wasn't there either. Virginia sagged against the door frame. "Oh God, please," she prayed, fighting panic. She went back to the labor room.

"She's gone, Stella. I think she's in the barn!" she sobbed.

Miss Evans stood up straight as a soldier. "God has not given us the spirit of fear, Virginia, but of power and of love and of a sound mind. There must be a way—"

Virginia's hysteria subsided. "A way—a way, oh, oh, yes, there *is* a way." She ran outside and tore at Paul's arm. He was futilely trying to keep the blaze contained.

"Beth," Virginia panted, "I think she's in the barn!"

Paul looked back at the fire in horror.

"There's another way in—hurry!"

They ran together back to the house and through the kitchen. Furball tried to follow them into the woodshed. Virginia led the sheriff to the trapdoor behind the pile of wood. They climbed down into the cool darkness of the tunnel.

In the bedroom, Shannon clung to Miss Evans. The old woman wiped a damp cloth across the girl's forehead, then across her own.

"It'll be over soon," Miss Evans promised.

"I'm so afraid," Shannon whispered. "I don't want my baby to be dead."

A siren wailed in the distance. "The ambulance is coming," Miss Evans said. Relief was obvious in her voice.

"I want to push!" Shannon cried.

"Oh, help!" the old lady cried and jumped to action.

The ambulance drove around to the back of the house. The two attendants were confused by the blaze now reaching the roof of the old barn.

"I thought this call was about a baby," one of them said. They knocked on the back door and hearing nothing, walked into the house. Shannon's cries drew them to the bedroom.

"Praise the Lord! You're here!" Miss Evans exclaimed.

"I'll get the stretcher," one of the medics said.

"No time!" Miss Evans declared. "Wash up. This baby's coming—right now!"

Shannon gasped and grabbed one of the attendant's arms. "Miss Evans, I'm sorry I was so nasty—I—"

"Come on, honey!" Miss Evans cheered. "Push! You're just about done!"

The other medic stood by Miss Evans, assisting. "You're doing great!" he told Shannon. "And you're not doing too bad either, Grandmother."

Miss Evans shot the young man a quick smile. "This baby's early," she told them. "You boys better get ready to go here."

The next contraction had the baby born. The tiny little boy wailed weakly. Miss Evans's skilled hands wrapped the infant. The attendant stepped in to finish helping Shannon.

Miss Evans showed the wee bundle to the girl. Shannon eased her grip on the other attendant. He rubbed his arm. "You ought to take up wrestling," he said.

Shannon laughed weakly and reached out for her child. She looked at the infant closely. "I'm glad now—I didn't know . . ."

Miss Evans patted her arm. "Of course you didn't know. What a beautiful little life!"

Miss Evans suddenly reached out for the bedpost to support herself. She looked at the paramedics and smiled weakly. "I'm feeling a little woozy—I think I need to lie dow—"

One of the men caught her as she collapsed. He looked at his partner. "We'd better take them all in."

At the end of the underground tunnel, Paul pushed open the trapdoor and helped Virginia up the ladder. Smoke filled the tack room. Their eyes watered and they gasped for air.

Paul led the way into the barn. The horse was screaming in panic. Beth was in the stall, trying to untie the halter rope while dodging the flying hooves.

She was covered with grime, and burning cinders had charred her blouse in several places.

"Nutmeg, stop! I want to help you! I want to help you!" she kept saying.

Paul pulled the girl out of the way and pushed her toward her mother. Pieces of burning roof began falling around them.

Paul grabbed an empty grain sack and ripped it open. He tied it over the horse's eyes and gripped the halter tightly as he untied the horse. He backed Nutmeg out of the stall.

"Get back to the house," he shouted to Virginia. He was about to swing on the horse's bare back when a burning board fell and struck Virginia down. Paul handed the halter rope to Beth and pushed the burning fagot away. Virginia was unconscious.

Nutmeg was almost impossible for the girl to hold and the roof was about to collapse. Paul grabbed Beth around the waist and lifted her onto the horse's back.

"You've got to ride her out of here," he shouted above the roar of the fire. "She can't see the flames, so head straight out the front. Just hug her neck and kick her hard. You'll go right through."

He put the halter rope in her hands. Beth gave him a brave smile.

"Now git!" the man shouted and slapped the horse smartly on the rump.

Nutmeg jumped forward with Beth clinging to her back, urging her on. They headed right toward the wall of flames.

Joey led his father through the house and into the woodshed. They climbed up the broken stairs to the little room. Joey climbed into the crawl space. He was handing his father sacks of the cocaine when Gautier found them there.

"So! Now we know," the Frenchman said quietly. "I told my partner it was in this house somewhere." He pulled the stiletto out of its sheath and touched the tip to his finger. He crouched and advanced across the room. Vince threw his partially filled gunnysack in the man's face and dove for the knife. The men crashed on the floor and struggled for control of the weapon.

Joey, in the crawl space, was paralyzed with fear. He wanted to go to his father's aid, but found he could not move. He lay his head in his arms and tried to breathe. Every blow he heard seemed to fall on him.

Vince's strength was equal to Gautier's superb physical condition. The men tumbled down the broken stairs and landed on the rough plank floor of the woodshed.

The bags of cocaine spilled out of the gunnysack, bursting open.

"It is stupid to die for what doesn't even belong to you!" Gautier snarled. He was tensed, ready to leap at Vince the first chance he could.

"It's mine!" Vince snarled back. "All of it!"

"You are a dead man," Gautier snapped and dove for the knife. He and Vince clashed and struggled. Gautier kicked the slower man down and poised for his final lunge.

A flying figure tackled the Frenchman around the knees, bringing him down to the dirt. Paul had come out of the tunnel behind the stack of wood and heard the men fighting.

As the sheriff was subduing the startled

Gautier, Daggett rolled out of the way and staggered out the door, through the kitchen and out of the house. Paul locked Gautier's arms painfully behind his back and snapped the handcuffs in place.

"A magazine writer, eh? For a nonexistent magazine." He pulled the man to his feet and guided him outside to the patrol car.

On his way back to fetch Virginia out of the tunnel, he spotted the spilled contents of the sack among the wood. He tasted a pinch of the white powder.

"I guess this explains everything," he murmured.

He found Virginia sitting up at the bottom of the ladder in the tunnel. She was holding the bloody bump on her head. "Is Beth okay?" she asked.

"I saw her just now, by the ambulance," Paul assured her. He helped her to her feet and out into the woodshed. "Look at this," he said. "Cocaine, and there's bound to be more around here somewhere. I've got Gautier in custody out in the patrol car."

"Mr. Gautier?" Virginia was appalled. "You mean he was—?"

"I'm sure he had a big stake in this." Paul led Virginia out to the backyard. The paramedics were carrying Shannon and the baby out of the house on a stretcher. The sheriff and Virginia followed them to the ambulance. As they reached the vehicle the barn's walls collapsed with a thundering crash. Sparks flew everywhere. Smoke now also spiralled up from the roof of the house.

"Stella!" Virginia cried when she saw the old woman lying in the ambulance.

Miss Evans waved her hand. "Now, don't fuss. I'm fine. Just too much excitement all at once. These young hoodlums are taking me in for observation now that I've done all their work for them. Makes 'em feel better about standing around watching me work in there." She winked at the attendant nearest her.

Beth stood by the ambulance with Nutmeg trailing by the halter rope. Her face was streaked with grime and looked white underneath all the soot.

"I'm sorry, Shannon," she said faintly, trying to get closer to the stretcher. "I—I didn't think—I never thought you'd . . ."

Shannon reached out for her free hand. "I guess I asked for it," she said weakly. "Guess I ask for trouble sometimes."

"Is your baby alright?" Beth asked, trying to see it.

"He's fine. It's going to be alright, Beth."

"That's what Miss Evans said," Beth remembered. Tears streaked down her dirty face.

Shannon smiled weakly across the ambulance at the old lady. "She was right. I think she's been right about a lot of things lately."

The paramedics got the stretcher secured in the vehicle and shut the doors. The red lights and siren came on and it drove away. The sound of another siren blended with it as the volunteer fire department came down the county road.

The firemen quickly set to work dousing the flames that were eating away at the roof of the house. The barn was no more than a pile of burning rubble.

Virginia took Beth in her arms. "I'm so thankful you're alright!" Beth hugged her mother tight and buried her head in her mother's embrace.

Paul radioed his headquarters from the patrol car. "Moran? Put out an all-points bulletin on Vince Daggett. We've got a narcotics operation here."

No one noticed the pale face looking down at them from the chamber window.

CHAPTER 10

From the window, Joey watched the different vehicles depart. The sheriff took Virginia with him into town to get her car while he took Gautier to jail. Joey saw the fire fighters stow their gear and leave also. The old house seemed quiet, as though she held her breath, waiting.

"I'm sorry I ever told Dad about this place," Joey moaned. "It was wrong to bring it here—"

Downstairs a door slammed and Furball yelped and barked as though in play. Then all was quiet once more. Joey walked over to one of the big pillow cushions and sat down, holding his head in his hands. He felt drained, hollow.

After a while, smells of hot food broke into Joey's troubled thoughts, reminding him of his own hunger. He started crawling back through the tiny passageway when he realized he had no safe way of escape.

The other end of the tunnel is probably blocked now, he thought. *And I can't go through the kitchen*. His realization made him return to the storage chamber. He cracked open the door to the hall. The upstairs seemed deserted.

Silently he made his way along the hall and downstairs to the parlor. It too was empty. As he passed the piano he touched it gently. Suddenly Furball barked from the parlor door and bounded into the room. His rib cage was still encased in bandages and he wore a patch over one eye. He leapt at Joey, knocking him against the keyboard.

"Furball!" The boy forgot himself and tussled with his dog.

"Joey! How did you get in here?" Beth stood at the parlor door with her hands on her hips. Her face was bruised and she had bandaged some of her cuts. "Mom locked all the doors."

Joey struggled for an explanation.

Beth warily crossed the room, wrestling with her thoughts. "Were you part of all this?"

Joey's eyes begged her to stop. The silence stretched between them.

"You know about that awful cocaine stuff, don't you? And the barn. You knew Nutmeg was in there," Beth started crying. "How could you?"

"No! I didn't do it! We didn't know . . ."

"I liked you, Joey Daggett. I saved your dog for you! And now you try to hurt us . . ." She ran through the parlor to her bedroom.

Furball sat at Joey's feet and cocked his head.

Joey buried his face in the dog's fur. "I don't know what to do anymore," he said dully. He stood up and turned to the dog, "You stay, boy. You're safe here." Then he turned to let himself out the front door and closed it carefully behind him. He stood a moment on the porch looking at the old house, then ran slowly down the steps and into the woods.

Joey slowed to a walk once the trees surrounded him. He shoved his fists in his pockets and dropped his chin to his chest.

Snow whispered through the trees. The boy stopped by a big pine and leaned against it to listen. He stood there a long, long time.

When Joey finally arrived at his own yard he saw the headlights of an approaching car. He moved back into the shadows. Night came quickly in the winter and the cold was biting. He yearned for the warmth of his bed and the forgetfulness of sleep. He rubbed his cheeks to get them warm, but the coldness remained. It seemed to come from somewhere inside of him.

The car came toward the house. Joey stepped out of sight behind some trees. He watched a man in uniform step out of a county patrol car and walk to the door. Joey crept closer to get a better look. He could see that the man wasn't Sheriff Larsen, and he was relieved.

He slipped around to the back of the house. A window pane in the kitchen door was broken. He crouched beside it and watched.

"So there's no problem getting it out, eh?" the man said. "There's an APB out on you right now, Daggett. If I wanted to, I could—"

Daggett tensed. "I can get it, I tell you! How was I to know that Frenchman was around?" Vince moved into Joey's line of vision. He had a knapsack packed, ready to leave. "The sheriff has that fellow out of the way now," he added.

"Where is it, Daggett?" Moran demanded.

Vince tightened the strap on the sack. "So you and Osborne can go halves? Forget it! You're smarter than that, Moran."

Joey could see the deputy sheriff come into the kitchen. "I ought to arrest you right now," the big-jowled man threatened. "Nobody'd believe you. You've got no leverage around here, Daggett, and I've got plenty!"

Moran made a move to unholster his gun, but he had miscalculated his adversary. Vince threw himself across the room. The gun flew out of the deputy's hand and the two big men grappled on the floor. Joey could hear the crash of dishes and the grunts and thuds of blows. He struggled with the door and looked around frantically for something to use to break it open. Then from the corner of his eye, he saw movement in the trees across the clearing. Someone was there, watching. Joey froze. He heard a sharp thud inside the house and the sound of a body falling to the floor. Vince burst from the kitchen door, knapsack in hand, nearly stumbling over his son.

"Dad, there's someone over there, behind those trees."

Vince looked where Joey pointed. "I'm going to the mine," he whispered. "I'll lose him if he tries to follow. You'd better get lost too. Git me some food. I gotta think . . ." Vince darted into the woods and became one with the darkness. Joey hardly heard his father's footsteps in the snow.

The boy ran into the woods and stood shivering. He saw a light go on in his house. Moran must be conscious. Joey jogged back through the woods toward the Cooper's house. He could see that Virginia had returned with the car. He stood behind the big rock north of the yard and stared at the warm yellow light beckoning him from the windows. It looked so welcoming, and so out of reach. The snow continued falling around and upon him. He curled up beside the rock and wondered if he'd ever be warm again.

The cold woke him after only a few hours of sleep. He was so cramped from the cold he could hardly straighten up. The night was moonless, and in the pitch dark Joey could see live coals still glowing from the charred remains of the barn. His numb feet felt full of needles as he staggered across the yard.

He found a stick and uncovered a bed of coals. His hands lost their stiffness in the warmth. The only section of the barn that still stood was part of one wall of the tack room. Joey looked back at the house, but it was dark and sleeping.

Fallen beams from the roof lay in a tangle. He climbed over them carefully. Several times the burned wood gave way beneath his weight. He figured out where the trapdoor should be. The spot was covered with a pile of debris. He started clearing it away and soon his hands were as black as the night.

He was about finished when suddenly he fell

through the flooring and into the tunnel. The bottom was covered with slushy ice from the water the fire fighters had sprayed over the barn that afternoon. Joey was soaked with it. He ached with the penetrating cold.

When he climbed into the woodshed at the other end, Furball rose from his bed behind the wood stove in the old kitchen and started scratching at the woodshed door.

"Hush!" Joey whispered as he opened the door slowly. Furball leapt up and licked his face. Joey closed the door carefully and took the dog with him as he climbed the broken stairs in the woodshed and went across the tiny room above.

Joey hardly noticed the cache of white powder as he passed it in the crawl space. Once in the chamber, he took off his wet clothes and curled up on the rug. Furball lay down beside him and the boy luxuriated in the newfound warmth. He slowly relaxed and fell into a deep sleep.

Chuck Warren drove out to the boarding house the next morning. "Is Beth handy?" he asked Virginia right away.

She brought him in and set coffee and hot rolls in front of him. Beth sat at the table doing homework.

"Shannon is fine," he told her.

Relief flooded the girl's face. "I prayed like Miss Evans told me," she said.

"What about the baby?" Virginia asked, sitting beside him.

"He's okay too. They both have to stay in the hospital for awhile, but they're going to be fine.

Shannon's folks are flying in tonight."

"And your great-aunt?"

"Was released this morning," Chuck replied as Mrs. Cooper refilled his coffee cup. "She's at my place now. She needs rest. Maybe you need some too. I'll take some of her things to her."

Virginia nodded. "There's certainly no guarantee she'd get any rest around here."

Beth felt herself shrinking away from the look on her mother's face. Virginia sat down again and pressed her forehead. "I wonder if this boarding house idea was such a good one."

Chuck fiddled with his cup. "Are you really sorry you opened your doors? My aunt's talking about coming back. She's been real happy here—she felt needed and loved."

Virginia paced to the dining room window and stared out at the smoldering remains of the barn.

"It's all so uncertain," she said, her back to her guest.

"And you'd rather go back to where you are sure of each day, where nothing and no one can upset your plans?" Chuck's tone was kind, but Virginia did not respond.

"We've got to stay, Mom!" Beth insisted. "I have Nutmeg and—"

Virginia clenched her fists. "That horse has nothing to do with this, Beth. I am sick to death of trouble! And that horse almost cost you your life yesterday!"

Beth cowered under her mother's anger.

"It seems to me," the woman went on, "that you'd better get your values straightened out, young lady!"

Chuck got to his feet. "Maybe that's the real issue, Virginia," he said gently. "Deciding what's important."

Virginia walked him to the front door without a word.

Beth tried to keep out of her mother's way all day. Late in the afternoon she couldn't stand staying in the house any longer.

"May I take Nutmeg out for a ride?" she asked meekly.

Mrs. Cooper was sitting at her desk, looking over the bills. "Where will you be?"

"I thought I'd go down to the lake and back. Maybe I'll spot a good Christmas tree." She gave her mother a hug.

"Just be sure you're home in time for supper."

Beth stopped in the kitchen to pull on her boots. She looked around for Furball. "He must've gotten out," she figured.

The December sky was full of clouds. Beth was glad she'd bundled up; the cold air even penetrated her heavy woolen pants.

"But it's so pretty out here!" she told the horse. Nutmeg perked up her ears. "How can Mom even think about moving away?"

Soft snow began to fall. Flakes fell on the horse's heavy winter coat. Beth looked at the snowflakes on the back of her mitten. "Mr. Warren says every one of them is different. Isn't that something?"

Beth sat there on her horse in the middle of the lane looking at the delicate icy patterns. Snow blanketed the world around her. No outside noise interrupted the soft sounds.

"I didn't know you could hear it snow," she whispered. "I wonder what it's saying."

Nutmeg snorted.

"I love you too, God," she whispered back to heaven. She stuck out her tongue and felt the snow melting on it. A sudden sadness passed over her. "Please help Joey," she prayed.

Nutmeg pranced impatiently and they set off again. As they neared the cow path to the old gully, Beth began looking at evergreen trees. She saw a good one back along the path and dismounted to take a look at it. She tied Nutmeg to a tree.

"O Christmas tree, O Christmas tree," she sang as she wandered from one tree to another. Her search drew her farther and farther down the path.

At the edge of the gully she stopped short. A camp fire burned near the mouth of the mine. "Golly, who's there?" She turned and started quickly back up the path. She did not hear the man come up behind her. A heavy, gloved hand clamped over her mouth and a strong arm lifted her off her feet. She was carried back down the path.

Beth tried to scream and kick herself free, but the arm only squeezed her tighter, forcing the breath right out of her.

Oh, Jesus, Jesus, help! she prayed over and over as consciousness slipped away.

Sheriff Larsen and Deputy Moran arrived at the boarding house after Beth had left for her ride.

They had an official search warrant with them.

"You don't need that," Virginia said when Paul handed it to her. "You know I want this cleared up as much as you do."

"There's probably a large haul of cocaine here," Paul told her. "Gautier was wanted in Florida for smuggling narcotics. Those boys don't usually fool around with anything small."

The men shed their heavy coats and set to work. Virginia followed Paul, watching him. Dusk passed unnoticed as the snow continued to fall outside.

"You'll stay for supper, won't you?" she asked Paul. The two of them were in the little room over the woodshed. She glanced outside. "Beth should have been back by now." Worry crept into her voice.

"Where is she?" Paul asked.

"Riding down the lane toward the lake. She sometimes rides down into that gully by the mine, but she knows not to go in there. You don't think there's anything wrong—"

Paul shook his head. "I don't like it. Not with some of these characters still out loose."

Joey had slept far into the afternoon. Furball's restlessness had wakened him and Joey let the dog out into the upstairs hall.

Smells of food assailed him. Only the memory of the dark figure in the woods beside his house, and Deputy Moran's threats against his father, kept him from wanting to go home.

As Joey lay hiding in the crawl space, his hunger gnawed his stomach like a rat in a cage. In the early evening he dozed off and didn't hear Furball scratching at the chamber door.

Sounds of voices in the little room at the other end of the crawl space jerked Joey awake. He recognized the sheriff's voice, and Mrs. Cooper's. He inched carefully backwards into the storage chamber. He was about to stand up when the chamber door opened. Furball ran in, followed by a man.

The snow-filled clouds outside allowed little light to filter through the chamber windows. Joey finally recognized Deputy Moran and crawled quickly back into his hiding place. Furball headed straight in his direction.

Joey was near the false back of the cupboard when he heard Mrs. Cooper's concerns about Beth. "Not near the mine!" Joey whispered in dismay.

He heard the sheriff and Mrs. Cooper leave the little room. He waited a moment then pushed away the false back of the cupboard and crawled out. He looked back at the cache of cocaine. Furball had entered the crawl space from the chamber end and was already halfway through. Deputy Moran beamed a flashlight into the hole.

"Take it! Go ahead and take it!" Joey cried. He ran across the little room and down the broken stairs. He surprised Sheriff Larsen and Virginia as he burst into the old kitchen and darted past them, with Furball at his heels. Boy and dog ran out the back door.

"Where—" Virginia stammered and looked back at the door to the woodshed.

"I'd better follow him," Paul said and watched Joey disappear at a run into the woods.

"I'm coming!" Virginia announced, her jaw set. She pulled on her winter boots and noticed Paul watching her with approval. "I put away my high heels a long time ago," she said.

Paul went to the stairs in the dining room and called to Moran. "Stay here and keep looking. I should be right back."

"Right," Moran called down. "It's bound to be here somewhere." Moran listened to the door slam shut downstairs and heard the jeep drive away. "Take your time," he whispered and smiled. He held a sack of dangerous white powder in his hands.

CHAPTER 11

Joey knew a shortcut to the gully. Even in the dark he made his way quickly. The freezing night air cut into his lungs. He keenly felt his lack of food. The cold dulled his pain though, as he plowed through the drifts. Having Furball beside him was his only comfort.

When he finally neared the rim of the gully he slowed. He saw the flicker of the camp fire. Very slowly he inched over the rim of the gully and began sliding down toward the bottom. The snow was soft and he moved noiselessly.

Joey was near the mouth of the mine when he saw Beth. Her hands were tied behind her and she sat just inside the mine shaft. Vince was crouched in front of the fire.

Joey hid behind an outcropping of stone. He

could hear Beth pleading. "You can let me go now, mister. I won't tell anybody you're here. Honest!"

"I told you to shut up," Vince snapped.

"But I want to go home now. My hands hurt and I'm cold. I won't tell—"

Vince didn't respond. His rifle was propped close beside him against a big rock.

"Look, mister, I have a great idea. You let me go, see, and then—"

Vince took two strides to cross the distance to the girl and slapped her across the mouth.

"I told you to shut up!"

The moment Vince struck Beth, a cry broke from Joey's lips. He ran to the rock, grabbed the rifle and aimed it at his father.

"Stop it!" he screamed. "Stop it!"

Vince whirled around to meet the new attack. "Joey!" he cried out in surprise. Beth gasped. Joey didn't move.

"Hey, kid," his father said. "it's me, your old man." Vince tried to read his son's face. "Give me the gun."

"Untie her!" Joey ordered.

"What?" Vince moved toward Joey and the boy jerked the rifle to point at his father's chest.

"I mean it, Dad. You're crazy. This cocaine stuff, the money, it's made you crazy. You don't care about anything anymore." He choked on a sob, but held the gun steady.

"Joey, there's no time for this! Moran has a buyer! Do you understand? We're gonna be rich! I've got a plan on how to get the stuff out—"

"Moran already has the cocaine. He's up at the house now."

"What?" Vince roared. He charged the boy. "You must've told him where—"

"Joey!" Beth screamed. "Behind you!"

A short, dark figure loomed up suddenly behind Joey and knocked the boy down hard. Vince stopped short and backed toward Beth. The man held a knife and looked as though a flick of his wrist would send it flying to its target. He took the rifle from Joey's limp hands and pushed the unconscious boy aside with his foot.

In that moment Vince grabbed for Beth and held her in front of himself. The wiry man smiled and aimed the rifle at the girl. Beth blanched.

"You think the girl matters to me?" he asked. "I would have to kill her anyway, you idiot. Did you really think you could get away with so much of our property? You are a fool, Vince Daggett. Gautier told me last week you were the one to watch."

The man had a rifle aimed at Beth's stomach. Suddenly Joey stirred at the man's feet. He swung the rifle down at the boy.

"No!" Beth screamed. With a terrible cry Vince thrust Beth aside and lunged across the camp fire at the man. A shot rang out.

Beth landed on her shoulder at the mouth of the mine. Pain shot down her arm. She saw Vince crumble to the ground.

Gautier's partner had fallen back under Vince's attack and when Joey tried again to rise to his feet, the man swung the rifle butt to strike him again.

A chilling animal snarl was the only warning of the next attack. Furball leaped from the rock outcropping and lunged for the man's throat. The rifle dropped to the snow as the man struggled to protect his jugular vein. He screamed in terror as the wolf-dog ripped the sleeves of his jacket and tore at him with murderous intent.

Beth worked her hands against the ropes. She heard someone shouting her name from back up the path.

"Mom! Mom!" she screamed in reply.

The Frenchman found his knife. It flashed in the light from the fire.

A gunshot split the air. "Hold it right there!" Sheriff Larsen cried out. "Throw the knife aside," he ordered.

Joey moaned and sat up. He called Furball to him. The Frenchman obeyed the sheriff's order. Paul Larsen stepped into view from the edge of the path and Virginia came out right behind him. She ran immediately to Beth.

All became quiet. The gully looked like a battle-field. Joey held the still snarling dog; the French-man's clothes were torn to shreds and his hands and face were scratched and bleeding from the dog's sharp fangs. Vince Daggett lay in a pool of blood near the fire.

"Go back to the jeep and radio for an ambulance. Then drive back to the house for Moran," Paul ordered Virginia.

"No," Joey called, struggling to stand erect. "Moran's in on it—"

Virginia stopped.

"Are you sure of that, Joey?" Virginia asked. The sheriff got the Frenchman handcuffed and pulled him aside.

"How do you know such a thing?" Paul probed. Beth watched the anguish on Joey's face. The boy stumbled across the clearing and picked up his father's rifle from the snow. He looked at it in his hands.

"I—I tried to stop him. I almost shot him!" he said. His chest heaved with emotion as he threw the gun into the woods. He staggered to his father's body. "Dad?" he whispered. Vince stirred. The sheriff knelt beside the man and looked at the wound.

"It's bad, son," he said gently to Joey.

Tears rolled down the boy's face. Beth and Virginia stood by, watching helplessly. Furball sat beside his master.

"It was never worth it—" Joey said, crying. He looked up at the sheriff. "I tried and tried to tell him, but he wouldn't listen, so I helped him."

"Radio for the ambulance, Virginia," Paul said. "We'll take care of Moran later."

Joey rocked his father in his scrawny arms. "I told him about the hiding place in your house. I didn't know you—" he looked at Beth through his tears. She smiled at him as best she could. Furball sniffed Vince's body and whined.

Virginia returned from the jeep with a blanket and covered the wounded man. She knelt in the snow beside Joey. Paul took off his coat and then his shirt. He tore the shirt into strips and used them to stanch the flow of blood from Vince's wound. Snow was still falling. It had already softened the evidences of struggle and violence at the campsite.

A log hissed in the camp fire as Beth threw on

more wood. The sparks flew upwards into the snow-filled sky. "Oh, God," she whispered. "How come there's so much trouble?"

Vince moaned. His eyes wavered open. "Joey?" he called weakly.

The boy wiped the snow off his father's beard. "Yeah, Dad."

"I'm sorry about—about the dog."

"It's okay, Dad—look, he's alright." Furball came close and lay down beside the man.

"And the piano," Vince's breathing was labored. "It was a cussed thing to do." His eyes closed. Joey looked up at the sheriff in panic.

"He's resting," Paul assured him.

Snow filled the time and softened the vigil. Beth stood by the fire. A siren wailed faintly in the distance. Virginia jumped to her feet and went to the jeep to turn on the headlights.

Vince's eyes opened again. "Sure would like a chaw of tobacco—" he murmured.

"You'll be okay now, Dad," Joey promised.

"I never done right by nobody all my life—not yer ma, not you. I's always lookin' to get rich." He was gripped by a spasm of pain. He grabbed for Joey's hand. "Oh, God . . ." he gasped, then stopped.

The siren drew near and stopped. Virginia led the paramedics down to the gully. Joey stood back as the men worked over his father.

"We're losing him," one of them said. They worked frantically, moment after moment, snow-flake after snowflake.

"I'm sorry, sir," the young medic said to Paul.

Beth turned to Joey.

He and the dog were gone.

Two days later, Sheriff Larsen came by in his truck and knocked on the Cooper's back door. Nutmeg whinnied from her makeshift lean-to by the woodshed.

Beth answered the knock.

"Thought I'd come by and see how you are getting along now that life's so boring." He smiled at her. "It's a good day to go find a Christmas tree," he added when Virginia invited him in. Beth looked hopefully at her mother. Virginia nodded.

"Doesn't cost anything," Paul said. "You own hundreds of them."

The three of them walked slowly together down the lane. Beth pulled the sled behind her. She missed having Furball around.

"We caught Moran," Paul told them as they crunched through the icy snow. He carried an axe easily on his shoulder.

"He was over the border, fifty miles into Alberta with your car. The mounties have him. He had your car trunk full of cocaine."

"Is it over then?" Virginia asked weakly.

Paul put an arm around her shoulders and pulled her close. "Yes, it's all over."

Beth looked away.

"There were warrants out on Gautier's partner too," Paul went on. "We've shipped him back to Florida to stand trial. That dog really did a job on him," he added.

"But what about Joey?" Beth asked.

"I don't know. He is certainly mixed up in all this," Paul answered with a sigh. "I'm going to talk with the district attorney on Monday. I sure don't want to see him get sent to juvenile hall."

With Paul leading they turned off the lane to a stand of evergreens. They looked over several trees before settling on one. Paul chopped it down in just a few swift strokes.

"He was trying to help me," Beth said as she watched Paul tie the tree on the sled. She bit her lip in an effort not to cry.

The sheriff put an arm around her. "I know. That's the best thing that he has going for him. Keep saying your prayers, Beth. They seem to be working."

"Have you seen Joey since the night at the gully?" he asked as they headed back up the lane.

Beth shook her head. "I don't think anybody has. We went to his house. I left a note and asked him to come to us."

As they neared their house, Virginia looked puzzled. "I don't remember leaving so many lights on—"

They went in the door to the old kitchen and welcomed the warmth of the wood fire burning in the stove.

"Surprise!" several voices shouted. Miss Evans popped out of the dining room, followed by Chuck Warren and Shannon, leaning on the arms of a good-looking, older couple.

"Paul told us you needed cheering up, so we invited ourselves over for a tree-trimming party!" Chuck explained.

"I've got hot cider and popcorn all ready," Miss Evans added.

"So tell us where the decorations are," Chuck

finished, "and we'll get started."

Paul laughed at Virginia's surprise. "Tell me where the things are and I'll get them," he said.

Virginia gave him directions and started to lead them all into the parlor.

"Mrs. Cooper," Shannon stopped her to say, "these are my parents. Mom, Dad, these are the people I told you about, Beth and Virginia Cooper."

Virginia welcomed the handsome couple graciously. Mr. Dyer offered his hand to Beth.

"So you're the young lady with the horse," he said with a twinkle in his eye. Beth blushed and nodded sheepishly.

"Shannon can ride Nutmeg any time she wants," she offered. The big man laughed. Shannon leaned on her mother.

"Not this trip," the teenager said. "But thanks. Maybe when we come back."

Beth looked quickly at her mother.

The gathering in the parlor was a merry one. The Dyers were part of the fun. The men quickly had the tree secured on a stand and then gave way to the ladies with the tinsel and glass balls. Shannon stayed on the couch and watched. She looked happy, but tired and pale.

At last Virginia sat at the piano and played Christmas carols. Beth took some cider to Shannon. "I'm glad you came—"

"I wanted to see you again before we left for home. I wanted to thank you," Shannon replied.

Beth looked surprised.

"Tell your mother I've talked it over with my folks and we—I've decided to put my baby up for adoption." Shannon's voice quivered. "If—if he gets as good a home as you got, I'll be happy." She wiped her eyes.

Miss Evans stood near them. She handed Shannon a hankie. "You know, about this time of year a long time ago, God gave away a baby too."

Shannon nodded. "I know. I've been thinking about that. It helps to know that, somehow—"

Virginia was playing "Joy to the World" and everyone else was standing around the piano singing.

"It's funny," Shannon said, watching. "What must have hurt God so much—was joy—to the world."

"It'll be kind of like that for you too, dear," Miss Evans said. "You must never forget what that little boy will mean to the people who take him into their hearts and homes."

Before long the party began to break up. The Dyers were the first to leave. They shook Virginia's hand gratefully.

"We do hope we can come back under happier circumstances," Mrs. Dyer said as she left. "This is such a beautiful house. It's really lovely, just as you and your daughter are." She kissed Virginia on the cheek. "Thank you. You did us all so much good."

Paul and Chuck had been talking quietly in front of the fireplace. Chuck nodded his head to something Paul said, then he helped Miss Evans into her floor-length raccoon coat.

"I'm writing down every recipe I can remember," the old lady said as they left. "I can hardly wait to try out my pickle relish on you." She gave

Beth a big hug. "Keep my room warm. I'll be back with the new year."

The lights on the tree blinked off and on and the fire in the fireplace began to die down. Virginia took a pile of empty cider cups to the kitchen. Paul picked up the empty popcorn bowl and started after her. He stopped at the door to the living room.

"Chuck Warren is going with me to the hearing on Monday," he told Beth. "He's going to ask for custody of Joey."

Beth's eyes lit up. "Do you think he'll get it?"

"I don't know of a better man," Paul said with a smile, and left the room.

Beth sat staring at the fire. *Now if Mom'll just decide to stay!* She got up and headed for the kitchen too. She stopped still in the living room. She could see the sheriff standing under the mistletoe in the dining room kissing her mother.

"I'll bet we're staying!" Beth said with a giggle.

After the sheriff left, Virginia turned off all the lights except those twinkling on the tree and walked with Beth to her bedroom. Beth was glad to crawl beneath the covers. She watched the snow floating past her window.

"Do you think Joey'll come back?" she asked her mother.

"It's hard to tell," Virginia said as she sat on the edge of the bed. "He's got so much hurt and anger all mixed up inside of him. He's going to need time and plenty of love—"

"Shhh!" Beth interrupted. She sat up in bed

and listened. "Someone's in the parlor," she whispered.

She slipped out of bed and tiptoed to the bedroom door. Virginia was right behind her. Beth hardly dared breathe as she peeked out into the parlor.

In the flickering light from the Christmas tree she saw Joey on the piano bench. Furball was lying on the hearth. Joey blew on his hands and moved his fingers awkwardly across the keys. He began playing a Christmas carol and didn't see his audience standing in the doorway. Then Furball lifted his head and looked at them.

Joey glanced up and jumped to his feet.

"Oh, please, don't stop," Beth said. "It's such a pretty song." She walked across the room in her flannel nightie and stood by the piano.

Joey looked at her and at Mrs. Cooper. Virginia smiled and nodded to him.

Time hung many seconds in the room. Then Joey slowly sat back down on the bench.

"I know the words," Beth offered with a happy grin.

Joey rubbed his hands together and looked at Beth and her mother with a deep yearning in his eyes. The snow outside and the colored lights within gave a silent benediction as he began to play his music once again. The refrain echoed through the quiet old rooms. The old house seemed to take part in the song.

"Silent night," Beth sang, "holy night, all is calm, all is bright."

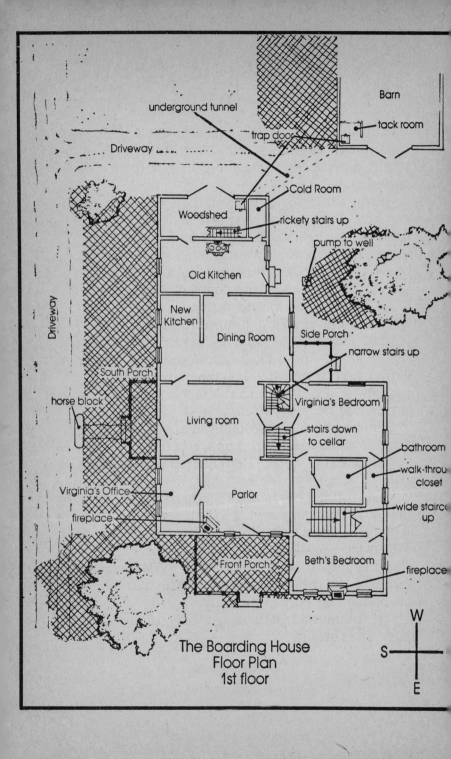

The Boarding House
Floor Plan
1st floor

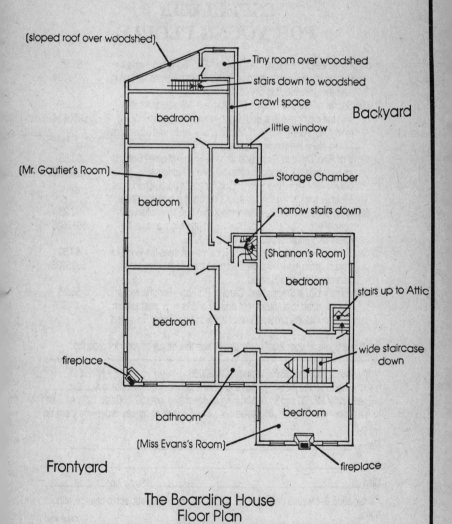

(sloped roof over woodshed)

Tiny room over woodshed

stairs down to woodshed

crawl space

Backyard

bedroom

little window

(Mr. Gautier's Room)

Storage Chamber

bedroom

narrow stairs down

(Shannon's Room)

bedroom

stairs up to Attic

bedroom

wide staircase down

fireplace

bedroom

bathroom

(Miss Evans's Room)

Frontyard

fireplace

The Boarding House
Floor Plan
2nd floor